grk
TAKES REVENGE

Joshua Doder

Andersen Press · London

First published in 2009 by
Andersen Press Limited
20 Vauxhall Bridge Road
London SW1V 2SA
www.andersenpress.co.uk
www.grkbooks.com

British Library Cataloguing in Publication Data available.

ISBN 978 184 270 661 9

Mixed Sources
Product group from well-managed
forests and other controlled sources
www.fsc.org Cert no. TT-COC-0002227
© 1996 Forest Stewardship Council
FSC

Typeset by FiSH Books, Enfield, Middx
Printed in the UK by CPI Bookmarque, Croydon CR0 4TD

Chapter 2

Tim loved his bed.

He had travelled round the world. He had walked on white beaches and trekked through thick jungles. He had swum through raging waterfalls and sailed round tropical islands. He had seen the Taj Mahal and the Sugar Loaf Mountain and the Empire State Building. But he wouldn't have swapped any of them for his own bed.

His duvet was warm and cosy. His room was quiet and comfortable. He could stretch out his arm and pick up a book, a comic, a game, a computer or a phone. What more could he possibly want?

In the school holidays, Tim often stayed in bed till lunchtime.

If he felt hungry, he went downstairs to grab a bowl of cereal or some toast, but he always came back upstairs again and ate his breakfast in bed. Then he read a book or played a game or just dozed.

This morning was different.

This morning, Tim was sleeping quietly, dreaming of this or that, when a hand pushed his shoulder and a voice demanded, 'Wake up!'

'Don't want to.'

'Come on! Wake up! You have to! It's important.'

'Sleep is important,' said Tim. 'Good night.'

He rolled over and snuggled deeper in his duvet.

He couldn't imagine why anyone would want to wake him up. It was the school holidays. He had nothing to do and nowhere to go. He just wanted to carry on dreaming.

But he wasn't allowed to.

He had barely settled his head on his pillow when the hand returned. And this time the hand didn't simply push his shoulder. No, it did something much, much worse. Without a word of warning, the hand grabbed Tim's duvet and pulled it off, exposing his head, neck and shoulders to the cold air.

Tim groaned, 'What are you doing?'

'I have to talk to you,' said the voice. 'Please, Tim. It really is important! You've got to wake up! I need your help!'

Tim groaned again. He knew who owned that voice. And he also knew that she wasn't the type of person who would take pity on a poor boy and let him stay in bed till lunchtime. He sat up, rubbing sleep dust from his eyes, and stared angrily at Natascha. 'What do you want?'

'Have you seen Max?'

'Not since last night,' said Tim. He leaned forward and peered at the other bed on the opposite side of the room. It was empty. He said, 'Have you looked in the loo?'

'He's not there,' said Natascha.

'Then he's probably downstairs having breakfast.'

'He isn't. He's gone.'

'Where?'

'I don't know,' said Natascha. She sounded panicky and frightened. She reached into the pocket of her

4

dressing gown and pulled out a sheet of paper covered with writing. 'I found this on my pillow. Max must have tiptoed into my room and left it there in the middle of the night.'

Tim glanced at the paper. 'What does it say?'

'Read it.'

'I can't.'

'Why not?'

'It's in Stanislavian.'

'Oh, I'm sorry,' said Natascha, shaking her head. 'I'm so worried, I can't think straight. Move up and let me sit down. I'll read it to you.'

Tim shifted sideways, making room on the edge of the bed for Natascha. She sat cross-legged and read the letter aloud, translating from Stanislavian into English as she went along.

This is what the letter said:

Dearest Natascha,

I would like to write a long letter to you, but I don't have time. So I will just tell you the facts. I have gone to kill Colonel Zinfandel.

I have been waiting a long time to take revenge on him. Now I have the chance to do it. I know where he is and I know what I have to do. So I have gone to find him.

I know you will want to come after me.

Don't.

I'll be safer without you. And you'll be safer at home.

5

Even if you wanted to find me, you won't be able to. So please don't even try. By the time you read this, I will be a long way away.

Don't be sad, Natascha. I am doing exactly what I want. If I'm killed, then you can be sure I'll die with a smile on my face.

Goodbye, my dear sister. Remember me as you remember our mother and our father.

Say goodbye to Tim from me. And thank his parents. They have been very kind to us.
With all my love,
Your brother,
Max

Natascha put down the letter and looked at Tim. 'You see?'

'Do you think it's true?' said Tim.

'Max doesn't lie.'

'He might be joking.'

'He would never make a joke about something like that.'

'I guess not,' said Tim. 'So you really think he's serious? I mean, do you think he'd actually kill someone?'

'Of course he would.'

'But he's only a boy.'

'That doesn't matter to Max,' said Natascha. 'He swore to take revenge on Colonel Zinfandel and he won't stop till he's done it. You have to remember, Tim, he's not like you. He doesn't believe in forgiveness. He believes in revenge. You know what they say in the

Bible? "An eye for an eye, a tooth for a tooth." Do you know what that means?'

'Of course I do,' said Tim, trying to sound more sure of himself than he actually felt. 'So what are you going to do about it?'

'Find him,' said Natascha.

'But he said in his letter—'

'I don't care what he said,' interrupted Natascha. 'If we don't find him, he's going to get himself killed. And I don't want my brother to die.'

Chapter 3

As you probably know, Stanislavia is a small, mountainous country in the part of Eastern Europe which is closest to Russia.

Natascha and Max Raffifi were both born in Stanislavia, but they spent their childhood travelling all around the world. They lived in Vienna, Montevideo, Riga, Toronto, Madrid and London.

Their father, Gabriel Raffifi, had worked for the Stanislavian Foreign Office. He had been the Stanislavian Ambassador to Austria, Uruguay, Latvia, Canada, Spain and the United Kingdom.

When the Raffifis were living in London, terrible things happened in Stanislavia. The president was thrown in prison and the country was taken over by a despicable despot named Colonel Zinfandel.

There are many brutal, unpleasant and cruel politicians in the world, but Colonel Zinfandel was one of the worst. He killed some of his enemies and imprisoned the others. The Stanislavian people didn't want him as their president, but they were too scared to protest. Using a mixture of terror, bribery and brute force, Colonel Zinfandel grabbed control of the country.

One of Colonel Zinfandel's oldest enemies was Gabriel Raffifi.

On the same day that he took control of Stanislavia,

Colonel Zinfandel sent his secret service to London. They kidnapped the Raffifis and took them back to Stanislavia, where they were put in prison. There, Mr and Mrs Raffifi were murdered.

If you want to know the whole horrible story, you should read *A Dog Called Grk*.

You will discover how Max and Natascha eventually escaped from prison and why they came to live in London with Tim and his parents.

You will also learn how Max made a solemn promise to his dead parents.

'I shall take revenge for your deaths,' he said. 'And I promise, Mother and Father, my revenge will be swift and cruel.'

Chapter 4

An eye for an eye, a tooth for a tooth.

Tim wrapped his duvet around himself and thought about revenge.

If you knew that a friend of yours was going to kill someone, what would you do?

Would you try to stop him?

What if he was intending to kill the man who had killed his parents? Wouldn't you let him do the one thing that he wanted more than anything else in the world? Even if that meant he might die?

Tim didn't know the answer to any of these questions. He didn't even know how to think about answering them. He wasn't a philosopher or a priest. He was just an ordinary boy who wanted to spend the whole morning in bed.

Given the choice, he wouldn't have done any thinking at all. He would have stretched out, pulled the duvet over his head, closed his eyes and gone back to sleep.

But he couldn't do that. Natascha was sitting on the end of his bed, waiting to hear his response. She was looking nervous, but determined. He knew what she was going to do: with or without him, she was going to go and search for Max.

'It's none of my business,' he could have said to her. 'If you want to help Max, then you're welcome to help him, but I'm not going to. He's your brother, not mine.'

Or he could have tried to argue with her. 'If Max wants to kill Colonel Zinfandel,' he could have said, 'why don't you let him? He's old enough to look after himself. Why don't you leave him alone and let him do what he wants?'

Or he could have said what an adult would have said: 'Max can't just go around killing people. Someone has to stop him. We'd better call the police. Pass me my phone, I'm going to call them right now!'

But he didn't say any of these things. If Max and Natascha needed his help, then he had to help them. That's what friends are for.

'Of course I'll come with you,' he said. 'Where are we going?'

Chapter 5

Natascha smiled for a moment, then sadness and worry settled over her face again. She slowly shrugged her shoulders. 'That's the problem,' she said in a quiet voice. 'I don't know where he is. I thought you might.'

'Me?' said Tim. 'Why me?'

'You share a room with him. Didn't he tell you where he was going?'

'He didn't tell me anything,' said Tim, shaking his head. 'This whole thing is a complete surprise to me.'

'You must know something,' insisted Natascha. 'Didn't he talk to you about travelling? Didn't he mention planes? Or trains? What about guidebooks? Or maps? Or tickets?'

'He didn't say anything about anything,' said Tim. 'You know what Max is like. He's good at keeping secrets.'

'He certainly is,' said Natascha. She sighed despondently. Then another thought occurred to her. 'I don't suppose you heard him leaving in the middle of the night?'

'No, I didn't.' Tim glanced across the bedroom at Max's bed. 'He was there when I went to sleep, but that's all I can remember. Sorry.'

'Oh, it's hopeless,' said Natascha. 'What am I going to do? How am I ever going to find him?'

Tim bit his fingernail. He always did that when he was thinking. And then he said, 'Maybe he left a clue.'

'What kind of clue?'

'I don't know,' said Tim. 'But it's still worth looking.' All thoughts of sleep suddenly forgotten, he threw aside his duvet, rolled out of bed and grabbed his dressing gown. He drew the curtains, letting light flood into the bedroom. 'Come on,' he said. 'Help me look.'

'What are we looking for?' said Natascha.

'We won't know till we find it,' said Tim. 'A ticket, a receipt, a guide book, a weather forecast – who knows? But as soon as we find it, we'll know it's exactly what we're looking for.'

Tim and Natascha searched the room for clues. They rummaged through Max's clothes and peered behind the chest of drawers and poked their fingers down the edges of the carpet. Tim crawled under Max's bed and emerged with a rolled-up sock. Natascha hunted through Max's cupboards and discovered a novel that she wanted to read. But neither of them found anything like a ticket, a receipt, a guidebook or a weather forecast.

In fact, after they had searched the entire room, they only discovered one thing which looked as if it might possibly be a clue and even that didn't appear to be much help.

When Tim tipped out the contents of the wastepaper basket, he found two plasters, a battery, an empty Coke can, a snapped pencil, an apple core, some orange peel, several tissues and a screwed-up piece of paper. He unrolled the paper and flattened it on the floor.

It was an ordinary sheet of A4 paper. One side was blank. In the middle of the other side, someone had written a single number and three words:

Zinfandel
Jules Verne
1

Tim showed the paper to Natascha. He said, 'Do you know what this means?'

Natascha peered at the paper. 'I've got no idea,' she said. 'But it's Max's handwriting.'

'Are you sure?'

'Of course I'm sure. I know my own brother's writing.'

Tim stared at the paper again. 'Zinfandel. Jules Verne. One.' He looked at Natascha. 'What do you think "Jules Verne" means?'

'It doesn't mean anything,' said Natascha. 'It's a name. Jules Verne was a real person.'

'Who was he?'

'A writer.'

'What did he write?'

'*Around the World in Eighty Days*,' said Natascha. 'And *Twenty Thousand Leagues Under the Sea*. And lots of other books, but I can't remember any of the titles.'

'I've heard of *Around the World in Eighty Days*,' said Tim. 'I think I might have seen the film. Do you know anything else about him?'

'He was French,' said Natascha. 'He lived about a

14

hundred years ago. He pretty much invented science fiction. That's all I know, really. We could look him up if you're interested.'

'I'm not,' said Tim. 'I'm just wondering why Max would be interested in him.'

'He wouldn't,' said Natascha. 'Max only reads books about tennis and football. He definitely doesn't like science fiction.'

'If he's not interested in Jules Verne, why would he write his name on a piece of paper? And why would he write Colonel Zinfandel's name there too? And what does the "1" mean?'

'I don't know the answer to any of those questions,' said Natascha. 'But I can tell you one thing for sure. It's not a clue.' She sighed deeply. 'Oh, this is hopeless. I'm never going to see my brother again.'

'You will,' said Tim. 'I'm sure you will.'

'You know that's not true,' sniffed Natascha. Tears were collecting in the corners of her eyes. 'He's going to try to kill Colonel Zinfandel – and he's going to die trying.'

Chapter 6

Tim looked at the trails of dried tears on Natascha's face and wished he didn't feel so useless. He hated seeing his friend suffering, but he had no idea how to help her.

He thought hard. There must be something he could do. But what? How could he find Max?

He stared at the piece of paper that he had found, wondering what the words could possibly mean.

Zinfandel
Jules Verne
1

What was the connection between Colonel Zinfandel and the writer of *Around the World in Eighty Days*? And why had Max written the number '1' with their names?

It didn't make any sense.

Tim folded the piece of paper and put it in his pocket. Natascha was right. It wasn't a clue.

There had to be another way to find Max.

Tim tried to recall anything unusual or unexpected that Max had said over the past few days, but he couldn't remember anything that gave any clue to where Max might have gone. He thought about what they knew and what they had discovered so far. And then he had an idea.

'Let's read the letter again,' suggested Tim. 'Maybe you missed something when you translated it from Stanislavian into English.'

'My translation was perfect,' snapped Natascha.

'I'm sure it was,' said Tim. He tried to sound calm and reassuring. He could see that Natascha was starting to panic. He didn't blame her; if his brother went missing, he would probably panic too. He said, 'Even if your translation was perfect, and I'm sure it was, you might have missed something. Maybe there's a clue in what he wrote.'

'I don't think so,' said Natascha. 'Max was very careful not to give away any useful information. He just said he was going to assassinate Colonel Zinfandel, that's all. He didn't say anything about where or when or how he was going to do it.'

Tim clapped his hands together. 'That's a clue!'

'What is?'

'If he's planning to kill Colonel Zinfandel, he has to be in the same place as Colonel Zinfandel.'

'Obviously.'

'So we just have to find out where Colonel Zinfandel is. And then we'll find Max.'

'You make it sound so easy.'

'It is easy,' said Tim. 'There's a magic box downstairs which has the answer to every question in the universe. All we have to do is ask.'

Chapter 7

Grk wasn't allowed upstairs.

He could go into the kitchen, the sitting room and the garden, but he was strictly forbidden from venturing upstairs and going into the bedrooms. That was the law in the Malt household.

Grk was the type of dog who didn't really care about laws. But he had learnt that breaking the law often had unpleasant consequences. He had been shouted at and sometimes even slapped. Once he had been locked in the garden for an entire afternoon. After that, he never went upstairs again. Unless he was alone in the house, of course. When everyone else went out, leaving him in charge, he roamed from the attic to the basement, treating the whole place as his own personal playroom.

Every night, Grk slept in a basket.

Every morning, he sat at the bottom of the stairs, his tail thumping on the carpet, waiting to greet people as they emerged from their bedrooms and came downstairs to have breakfast.

Mr Malt was usually the first person that Grk saw. Mr Malt liked to leave home as early as possible so he could get to work before his colleagues and prove how hard he worked.

Mrs Malt usually followed a few minutes behind her husband. She would rush downstairs to the kitchen, gathering her things for work, and drink the tea that Mr Malt had made for her.

During term time, the children would follow them soon afterwards. But in the holidays, the house stayed quiet for a long time after the Malts had drunk their tea, eaten their toast and gone to work.

Today was different.

Grk was a good guard dog. If he had ever heard burglars breaking into the house, he would have barked loudly enough to alert everyone in the street. But when he heard those feet on the stairs, he didn't bother barking, because he knew who owned them. He just sat at the bottom of the stairs, his tail wagging, wondering why Max was getting up so early.

Max came downstairs, knelt on the carpet, whispered goodbye to Grk and tickled his ears. Then he grabbed his coat and tiptoed out of the house, closing the front door silently behind him.

When Max had gone, the house was quiet again.

Not long after dawn, Mr Malt came downstairs, patted Grk on the head and went into the kitchen to make breakfast. He was soon followed by Mrs Malt. They drank their tea and ate their toast together, then went to work.

The house was quiet once more.

Right now, Grk was sitting at the bottom of the stairs. His head was cocked on one side and his tail was thumping on the carpet.

He could hear the sound of voices from the top of the

stairs. He knew the voices belonged to Tim and Natascha. Although he had no idea what they might be talking about, he did know two things for sure.

One: if they were talking, then they must be awake.

Two: if they were awake, then they would take him for a walk.

He sat at the bottom of the stairs, impatiently waiting and watching, hoping they would hurry up and come downstairs.

As the voices came closer and closer, his tail thumped faster and faster on the carpet. When Tim and Natascha finally reached the bottom of the stairs, Grk threw himself forwards, unable to contain his excitement, and hurled himself at their legs. Then he turned round and ran the entire length of the hallway, barking with excitement, ready to go out and smell the fresh air and throw himself into the new day.

When Grk got to the front door, he turned round once more and looked for Tim and Natascha, expecting them to be right behind him, eager to get outside as fast as possible.

To his disappointment, they hadn't grabbed their coats or put on their shoes. Instead, they had gone into the sitting room and sat down at the computer.

Grk trotted after them, wondering what they were doing. What could possibly be more important than going for a walk?

Chapter 8

Tim and Natascha pulled up two chairs and sat at the desk.

Tim switched on the computer, opened the browser and searched for 'Colonel Zinfandel'. He clicked on a link for news stories. The page showed the headlines from several news sites. Tim clicked on the most recent. The story had been updated within the past two hours and said that Colonel Zinfandel was currently visiting Paris.

'That was easy,' said Tim, feeling very pleased with himself. 'Colonel Zinfandel is in Paris. So Max must be there too.' He pushed back his chair and stood up. 'Shall we go and find him?'

'Paris is a big place,' said Natascha, staring at the screen and reading the news story. 'We can't just go there and hope we bump into Colonel Zinfandel. We'd have to know where to look.'

'No problem,' said Tim. He sat down again. 'Let's find him.'

He went back to the previous page and followed the other links to different news stories, but none of them revealed the exact location of Colonel Zinfandel. They simply said he was visiting Paris.

'I've got an idea,' said Natascha. She took over the keyboard and plugged three terms into a search engine: 'Stanislavia ambassador France.' She pressed RETURN and immediately found what she was looking for: the site of the Stanislavian Embassy in Paris. She started reading through the pages, searching for information.

Tim had no idea what she was reading. The site was written in a mixture of French and Stanislavian, and he couldn't understand either.

He had been to Stanislavia only once. During that brief trip, he met the president, flew a helicopter and escaped from a high-security prison, but didn't learn more than a couple of words of the language.

He had spent hours learning French at school, so he knew a few more words of that language. He could remember the meaning of '*pomme*', '*pain*' and '*fromage*', for instance. But the Stanislavian Embassy didn't have anything to say about apples, bread or cheese. So he simply stared at the pictures on the screen and waited for Natascha to translate whatever she had discovered.

She didn't take long. 'There,' she said triumphantly, pointing at the screen. 'Found it!'

'Found what?' said Tim.

'Colonel Zinfandel's schedule for the day.' Natascha leaned forward and peered at the small letters on the screen.

Tim stared at the screen too. He couldn't read what was written there, but he looked at the photograph of Colonel Zinfandel and remembered the day that the two of them had met.

Colonel Zinfandel was a handsome man with black

hair, a straight nose and lean cheekbones. Looking at him, you wouldn't have thought that he was a cruel dictator who had been responsible for the deaths of hundreds of his citizens and the misery of millions more.

'He's just going to Paris for the day,' said Natascha. 'He's arriving in the morning. In fact, he must be there already. He'll go straight from the airport to the Quai d'Orsay – whatever that might be – where he is going to meet the French Minister of Foreign Affairs. Then he's going to the Eiffel Tower, where he's having lunch at the Jules Verne Restaurant with a group of French business leaders. He'll visit the Paris arms fair in the afternoon and have more meetings with more business leaders. Then he's flying back to Stanislavia tonight.' She sighed. 'That's not much use, is it?'

'Wait a minute,' said Tim. 'What did you say? Where's he having lunch?'

'In the Eiffel Tower. I just told you that.'

'But where in the Eiffel Tower?'

Natascha looked at the screen and read what was written there. 'The Jules Verne Restaurant.' Her eyes widened. 'Where's that piece of paper?'

Tim dug into his pocket and pulled out the paper. He unfolded it and spread it out on the desk. He and Natascha stared at the number and the two words that Max had written there:

Zinfandel
Jules Verne
1

They looked at one another, suddenly excited by what they had discovered.

'That's it,' said Natascha. 'Jules Verne means the Jules Verne Restaurant.'

'And one must mean one o'clock,' added Tim. 'Max must have found out that Colonel Zinfandel is arriving at the Jules Verne Restaurant at one o'clock.'

They both grinned. Finally, they were on the right track. They knew where Max was going. And they knew when he wanted to get there. Now they just had to arrive first.

Natascha said, 'Can we get to Paris before one o'clock?'

Tim glanced at the clock in the corner of the computer screen. 'It depends on the trains. I don't know how long they take or when they leave. Let me look.'

Natascha moved aside, letting Tim take control of the keyboard. He went to the Eurostar website and searched for the times of trains running between London and Paris.

'There's a train leaving in half an hour,' said Tim. 'But we'd never get that one.'

'Why not?' Natascha pushed back her chair and jumped to her feet. 'We have to get there as quickly as possible. Come on, let's go!'

'It's just not physically possible,' said Tim. 'We're too far from St Pancras. We'd have to travel across half of London. We couldn't get there in half an hour.'

'When's the next train?'

'It leaves in . . .' Tim stared at the timetable on the screen. 'An hour and a half.'

24

'Could we catch that one?'

'We'd have to buy a ticket,' said Tim. 'And get from here to St Pancras. But if we're quick, we might just make it.'

'What are we waiting for?'

Chapter 9

Some people don't eat breakfast.

They jump out of bed, grab their clothes and plunge into the day on an empty belly.

Tim wasn't one of those people.

If he didn't eat breakfast, his stomach would start moaning and groaning by the middle of the morning, complaining to everyone within earshot. His arms would lose their strength, his legs would refuse to move and his brain would turn to jelly.

If he was going to spend the morning travelling to Paris, then searching for Max and Colonel Zinfandel, he had to have breakfast.

He sprinted downstairs to the kitchen, grabbed a bowl and a spoon, and poured himself some cereal. He sloshed some milk into the bowl, sat down at the table and ate fast. He knew he would probably get indigestion, but he was sure that a sore stomach is better than an empty stomach.

He ate the last mouthful of cereal, dumped his bowl in the sink and sprinted upstairs to his parents' bedroom.

He was hunting for his dad's spare credit card. He knew where it was kept. (In the top drawer of his dad's bedside table.) He also knew how angry his dad was going to be. (Very.) But he didn't have time to worry about anger, apologies or punishment now. Getting to Paris was the only thing that mattered.

He opened the top drawer of his dad's bedside table. Just as he had hoped, the credit card was lying among a jumble of receipts and coins. Tim plucked it out and shut the drawer again.

He hurried downstairs, sat at the computer, went to the Eurostar site and booked two tickets from London to Paris, leaving later that morning. The website told him to collect the tickets from St Pancras Station and reminded him to take the credit card that he had used to book the tickets.

He tucked the credit card into his pocket. Now he just needed three passports. And he was ready to go.

Mrs Malt kept useful documents in the tall filing cabinet beside the computer. Tim opened the top drawer and rifled through the files until he found one marked TRAVEL. He pulled it out.

Inside the file, he found several white envelopes. Mrs Malt had written on each of them in neat black capital letters. One said INSURANCE. Another said MONEY. And a third said PASSPORTS.

Tim looked inside the envelope that said MONEY. When Mr and Mrs Malt came home from their holidays or business trips, they dropped any spare change into this envelope. Tim sorted through the dollars, rupees and yen, searching for euros. He found a few and pocketed them, then closed the envelope and opened the one marked PASSPORTS.

There were five passports inside – and there should

have been six. One was missing. Max must have come here earlier this morning and taken his.

Tim grabbed three passports – his, Natascha's and Grk's – then put the file back in the cabinet and went to find the others.

While Tim was eating breakfast and buying tickets, Natascha had packed a rucksack with everything that they could possibly need for a trip to Paris.

This is what she put in her rucksack:

A bunch of bananas (in case they got hungry).

A bottle of water (in case they got thirsty).

A bar of chocolate (in case they ate all the bananas).

Some plasters (in case they got hurt).

A notebook (to keep notes).

Two pens (to write notes).

Two pencils (to write notes that could be rubbed out).

A rubber (to rub notes out).

A pocket English-French dictionary (to talk to French people and read French signs).

A book (to read on the journey).

Another book (in case she finished the first one).

A spare jumper (in case it got cold).

A blanket (in case it got even colder).

A spare lead for Grk.

She stuffed everything inside the rucksack. It was extremely heavy. She thought about taking a few things out, lightening the load, then decided not to.

You never know what you might need on a trip to Paris.

Now, Natascha was standing by the front door, holding her rucksack in one hand and Grk's lead in the other, wondering what had happened to Tim.

Grk was standing at her feet with his tail wagging quickly from side to side. He didn't know where they were going and he didn't care. He was just looking forward to getting out of the house and smelling the new day.

Natascha glanced at her watch. She was getting impatient. She had been waiting for a long time. When she finally saw Tim, she said, 'What's taken you so long?'

'I've been doing stuff.'

'What kind of stuff?'

'Important stuff. I've been buying tickets and getting passports and finding money and having breakfast.'

'Breakfast?' Natascha could hardly believe what she was hearing. 'We don't have time for breakfast! Don't you realise we're in a hurry?'

'I'm almost ready now.'

'Almost?' Natascha glanced at her watch again. 'We're going to be late. Come on, let's go. We have to leave this minute. Or we're going to miss our train.'

'I've just got one more thing to do,' said Tim. He turned round and ran towards the kitchen.

Natascha shouted after him, 'What are you doing? Hey! Tim! Come back! We have to go!'

29

Tim took no notice. There was one final thing that he had to do and he wasn't going to leave the house before he'd done it.

There was a shopping list stuck to the fridge. Tim took it off and turned it over. The back was blank. He placed it on the kitchen table and scrawled a quick note. This is what he wrote:

Dear Mum and Dad,
I have gone to Paris with Natascha and Grk.
Max is in trouble. We have to help him.
*   I have taken our passports and Dad's spare*
credit card and some euros too.
*   Sorry!*
*   See you later.*
*   Loads of love from Tim*

He put the note in the middle of the kitchen table where it couldn't be missed. When his parents came home from work that night, they would see it immediately.

Tim could imagine exactly what would happen next. His mum would cry. His dad would panic. They would be terrified that something terrible had happened to their son.

Tim didn't like the thought of his parents panicking. He wondered how he could make things easier for them.

He had an idea. He could add a few more sentences

30

to his note, explaining exactly why he was planning to go to Paris and what he was intending to do when he got there. He chewed the end of the pen and tried to think of the right words to say.

But before a single word could take shape in his mind, he heard Natascha's voice, shouting at him down the stairs. 'Tim! We're late! We're going to miss the train! What are you doing down there?'

Tim glanced at the clock on the wall and realised she was right. Unless they left now, they would never get to Paris. He dropped the pen on the table and ran up the stairs.

The front door was open. Natascha was pacing impatiently up and down the street, glancing at her watch and worrying about the time. As soon as she saw Tim, she said, 'What have you been doing? Don't you care about finding Max?'

'Of course I do,' said Tim. 'Sorry I took so long. Sorry I wasn't ready quicker. Sorry I didn't answer you when you shouted at me. Sorry I had breakfast.'

'Stop apologising so much,' said Natascha. 'You're wasting time and we don't have time to waste. Let's just go to Paris!'

She turned round and hurried along the street. Grk trotted by her side with his nose in the air, sniffing all the fascinating smells that the street had to offer.

Tim closed the front door. As the lock shut with a loud click, he remembered he hadn't brought a key. If they missed their train, they wouldn't be able to get back into the house. They would have to wander the streets till his parents got home from work.

There was no time to worry about that now. Natascha was already halfway down the street. If he didn't start moving now, she'd go to Paris alone and he would be left in London. He ran after her.

Chapter 10

They turned left, then right, and came to the main road.

A bus was approaching the bus stop.

'Run!' shouted Natascha. 'If we miss this, we'll have to wait hours for the next one!'

They sped down the street. Grk darted ahead of Tim and Natascha, his tail wagging and his nose in the air. For the first time that day, he was having fun.

They reached the bus and hopped aboard. Tim and Natascha pressed their oyster cards onto the reader.

The driver looked down his nose at Grk and said, 'Will that dog behave himself? I don't want any muck on my bus.'

'You don't have to worry about that,' said Tim. 'He's completely house-trained.'

'And bus-trained,' added Natascha.

'He's a very well-behaved dog,' said Tim. 'He's not going to pee on the floor.'

'He'd better not.' The driver glared at Grk.

Grk glared back. He didn't like people who didn't like him.

The two of them could have stayed like that for hours, glaring at one another, but further down the bus, people had already started grumbling. They were wondering what was taking so long. No one wanted to be late for work. The driver must have heard their grumbles, because he pressed a button to close the doors and said, 'Go on, then. Get inside. Just remember what I said. No muck on the bus!'

As Tim, Natascha and Grk hurried down the aisle to find a seat, the driver pressed his foot on the accelerator. The bus jerked forwards and joined the stream of traffic.

Five minutes and three stops later, Natascha, Tim and Grk jumped out of the bus, ran along the pavement and darted into the underground station.

Tim looked at a map on the wall to check their route. Natascha picked up Grk. As you probably know, dogs aren't allowed to stand on the escalators when they travel on the London Underground. They might get their claws stuck in the gaps. If that happened, they would lose their claws and possibly much more.

Tim and Natascha pressed their oyster cards on the reader, pushed through the ticket barrier and went down the escalator. When they reached the end of the escalator, Natascha put Grk on the floor and they hurried along the corridor to the platform.

There was a train waiting. It was packed with commuters. Natascha, Tim and Grk shoved themselves through the door and squeezed into the forest of satchels and suitcases and briefcases and rucksacks and backs and bellies and knees and elbows. There was hardly enough room for them, but they didn't want to wait for the next train.

When the doors closed and the train started moving, Tim found himself squashed between two fat men who smelt of sweat and onions. Natascha was flattened against a window. Things were even worse for Grk. Several people trod on him and not one of them apologised.

When the train finally arrived at King's Cross, passengers poured out onto the platform, sweeping Tim and Natascha and Grk out of the train with them. Luckily, King's Cross was where they wanted to get out, so they didn't have to fight their way back on. They allowed themselves to be dragged towards the exit by the flow of passengers.

When the crowds thinned, Tim, Grk and Natascha jogged down one corridor, then another, dodging round commuters, and reached the escalators. Natascha grabbed Grk in her arms and carried him to the top.

The escalators deposited the three of them in the ticket hall. They went through the barriers and followed the signs to St Pancras.

The high-ceilinged station was packed with people. A voice boomed from the loudspeakers, announcing arrivals and departures, telling passengers when the next trains left for Brussels and Paris.

Tim and Natascha looked around, wondering where to go next. Tim was the first to see a sign saying TICKET OFFICE.

'That way,' he said, pointing to the sign. 'Let's go and get our tickets.'

Natascha glanced at her watch. 'We're going to miss the train.'

'We'll be fine,' said Tim, trying to sound more confident than he really felt. 'We've got lots of time.'

35

In a lobby outside the ticket hall, Tim fed his dad's credit card into a silver machine. It groaned and moaned, then spat out two tickets.

They emerged from the lobby and hurried towards the platforms, following the signs that said EUROSTAR. Smart restaurants and fancy boutiques lined the station, but Tim and Natascha hardly even glanced at the window displays. They didn't have the time or the money to go shopping.

They showed their tickets at the barrier and took turns to pass through a metal detector, then joined the queue for Passport Control.

A man in a black uniform glanced at the photos in the back of Tim's and Natascha's passports, then checked the stamps in Grk's. He took a long look at the three of them. They stared back at him. Finally, the passport officer nodded.

'Have a good trip,' he said. 'Next, please!'

Tim, Natascha and Grk hurried onwards. They went up a long escalator which led to the platforms. Once again, Natascha held Grk in her arms till they got to the top. Then she put Grk on the ground and they jogged along the platform.

They stopped at carriage number 12. An inspector checked Tim and Natascha's tickets, making sure that they had come to the right place, then ushered them aboard.

'*Bon voyage*,' said the inspector. 'Have a good trip.'

'Thanks,' said Tim and stepped into the train. Grk leaped after him. Natascha came last.

They walked down the carriage and found their seats.

Natascha sat down. Tim sat opposite her. Grk crawled under his feet.

'We made it,' said Tim.

'Just,' said Natascha.

A couple of minutes later, the doors slid shut and the train eased out of the station.

Chapter 11

A voice came from the loudspeakers, booming along the entire length of the train, informing passengers that the journey to Paris would take two hours and twenty minutes. The buffet would open soon, said the voice, and would be serving all kinds of sandwiches and snacks as well as a full range of hot and cold drinks.

Natascha leaned forward and said, 'Are you hungry?'

'Not really,' said Tim. 'But I wouldn't mind something to eat. Shall we go to the buffet?'

'We don't have to,' said Natascha. 'We've got our own private buffet right here.' She opened the flap of her rucksack, took out some bananas and some chocolate, and shared them equally between Tim and herself. They ate slowly, savouring every mouthful.

Down on the floor, Grk was looking upwards, watching the bananas and the chocolate, hoping some crumbs might drop at his paws. But he was out of luck. Tim and Natascha ate every scrap, even licking their fingers and picking crumbs from the tabletop. They didn't know when they might eat again.

When their meal was over, Natascha pulled two books from her bag. She held them both in the air, showing the covers to Tim. One was called *Eagle of the Ninth* and the other was called *Emma*. 'Which do you want?'

'Don't mind,' said Tim.

'I want to read both, so I'll read whichever one you don't want. Pick one.'

'That one,' said Tim, pointing at *Eagle of the Ninth* because it had a picture of a Roman soldier on the cover. The other book had a picture of a smiling woman in a white dress and looked thoroughly boring.

Natascha slid *Eagle of the Ninth* across the table to him, opened the book in her hands and started reading.

Tim picked up his book and read the back. It sounded boring. He opened the cover and read the first few lines. It was boring. He closed the book and put it down on the table, then glanced at the floor.

Grk was curled by his feet. He wasn't fast asleep – he lifted his head whenever someone walked past – but he was taking advantage of the journey to get some rest.

That's a good idea, thought Tim.

He had been woken up far too early this morning. Now was his chance to catch up on lost sleep. He closed his eyes, leaned his head against the window and drifted into a deep, dreamless sleep.

Chapter 12

Colonel Zinfandel looked out of the window. Below him, he could see the sun, a blue sky and a landscape of white puffy clouds, stretching endlessly to the horizon. He said, 'It's a beautiful morning.'

'Yes, sir,' said the soldier standing opposite him. The soldier was wearing black shorts, a white T-shirt and a pair of blue boxing gloves.

Colonel Zinfandel was wearing white shorts, a black T-shirt and a pair of red boxing gloves. He said, 'Where are we?'

'Ten thousand metres above Switzerland, sir. The Alps are under those clouds.'

'How much further?'

'We'll be in Paris in thirty-five minutes, sir.'

'Perfect,' said Colonel Zinfandel. He turned to look at the soldier. 'That should give us just enough time. Are you ready to fight?'

'Yes, sir.'

'Then let's fight.'

In a single sudden movement, Colonel Zinfandel swung his right fist at his opponent.

The soldier was too quick for him. He ducked backwards, narrowly avoiding the blow, and darted across the ring.

Colonel Zinfandel sprang after him, swinging his left

arm this time, trying to land the first blow.

The two men paced in a circle, their arms raised, their eyes never leaving one another's faces. They were ten thousand metres above the ground, but they didn't think about that. All their attention was focused on the fight.

That morning, Colonel Zinfandel was flying from Stanislavia to France in his own private jet.

And that morning, just as he did every morning, Colonel Zinfandel was boxing.

His private jet was very versatile. His engineers had made sure of that. If he was tired, a bed could be made for him. The soft feather cushions and the thick mattress were as comfortable as the best beds in the best hotels in the world. If he was hungry, his chef would hurry to the kitchen and cook the type of meal that you would be lucky to eat in one of the world's finest restaurants. If Colonel Zinfandel wanted to do some exercise, three rows of seats would be removed from the middle of the plane and the space would be converted into a boxing ring.

Wherever he went, Colonel Zinfandel took his boxing gloves, his boxing shorts and his boxing shoes. He was always accompanied by several soldiers and body-guards. Every morning, he would pick one of them as his opponent.

Every morning, he would beat them.

Colonel Zinfandel loved boxing. He was a skilful boxer. Even more importantly, he was ruthless and cunning and determined to win.

No one had a hope against him.

41

The fight was short and brutal. Two minutes after they started, the soldier was lying on the ground with blood pouring from his nose and Colonel Zinfandel was hurrying back to his private rooms at the back of the plane.

He showered, dressed and breakfasted, then summoned his advisers and discussed what would happen when they landed in Paris.

Chapter 13

'Excusez-moi, Monsieur? Monsieur! Nous sommes arrivés!'

Tim opened his eyes. He didn't know where he was or what he might be doing there. He remembered going to sleep last night in his bedroom. He was sure it was still the school holidays. As far as he knew, he had nothing planned for today. Nothing, that is, apart from spending the whole morning in bed. So where was he now? How had he got here? Who was the woman leaning over him? And why was she speaking in a language that he couldn't understand?

'Monsieur, vous devez vous réveiller,' said the woman. She pointed out of the window. *'Nous sommes à Paris.'*

'I'm sorry,' said Tim. 'I don't speak French.'

'I know you don't,' said the woman.

As soon as those words came out of the woman's mouth, Tim recognised her as Natascha. And then he remembered everything. He sat up and looked out of the window. He could see a station platform, a guard in a black uniform and lots of passengers. A large sign read PARIS – GARE DU NORD. He said, 'We're in France!'

'That's why I woke you up,' said Natascha. 'Come on, you've slept enough. We've got to get to the Eiffel Tower.'

'How are we going to do that?'

'I don't know,' said Natascha. 'But let's go and find out. Or do you want to stay here? If you'd rather, you could just spend the whole day staring out of the window.'

'Yeah, that sounds like fun,' said Tim. He grabbed Grk's lead and clambered out of the seat. 'Okay, I'm ready.'

'Then let's go,' said Natascha. She slung her rucksack over her shoulder. Together, the three of them hurried down the aisle and went to the door. They stepped out of the carriage and joined the busy crowd of passengers on the platform streaming towards the exit.

The Gare du Nord is the busiest train station in Europe. It is always packed with people, catching trains to Holland, Belgium, Britain and Northern France.

Tim and Natascha stood in the middle of the concourse, looking at the busy crowds, wondering which way to go.

Voices boomed from loudspeakers, speaking in both French and English, telling passengers which trains were leaving from which platforms. People hurried from one side of the station to the other, carrying bags and pulling suitcases. Signs pointed in every direction, showing the way to buses and taxis and the métro. But not a single sign pointed towards the Eiffel Tower.

Tim felt completely confused. 'This is crazy,' he said, 'I've never seen so many people. What are we going to do? Where are we going to go?'

'That way,' said Natascha. She pointed across the station to a small blue booth marked with three words: *OFFICE DU TOURISME*.

'What does that mean?' said Tim.

But Natascha didn't hear him. She was already sprinting across the station, jumping over suitcases and dodging round passengers, hurrying towards the booth.

Tim couldn't read French, but he realised that the words printed on the booth weren't very different from their English equivalents. *'Office'* must mean 'office'. *'Tourisme'* must mean 'tourism'. And a tourist officer would be the perfect person to tell them how to find the Eiffel Tower.

Tim and Grk ran after Natascha.

The three of them reached the booth at the same time. A small blonde woman was sitting inside, filing her nails. Natascha put her elbows on the counter and said, 'Excuse me, do you speak English?'

'Of course,' said the woman. She had a strong French accent. 'I am the officer of the tourism, so I must have spoken English. It is obliged for my job. How can I help you?'

'We want to go to the Eiffel Tower,' said Natascha. 'How do we get there?'

'That is absolutely your choice,' said the blonde woman, continuing to file her nails as she spoke. 'You may take a taxi. Or you may take a bus. Or you may take the métro. Alternatively, if you so wish, you may use your own two feet and take a walk. As I said to you already, the choice is absolutely yours.'

Natascha said, 'Which is the best way to get there?'

'That depends,' said the blonde woman, putting the nail file on her desk. She picked up a tiny bottle of nail polish and unscrewed the lid. 'If you wish to exercise your legs, then it is advised to walk. But this might be tiring, because from here to the Eiffel Tower is a long way for walking. If you wish to be comfortable, then the taxi is the best. But this might be expensive. If you wish to save money, then you should take the bus.'

'We just want to get there as fast as possible,' said Tim.

'Then you must take the métro,' said the blonde woman. 'The métro is the quickest of the methods. And it is also not too expensive.'

'Where's the métro?' said Tim. 'Which way should we go?'

The blonde woman sighed as if she had never heard such a stupid question. She carefully replaced the lid on her nail polish, opened a drawer in her desk and pulled out a folded map. 'Here, I will show you exactly what you must do.' She unfolded the map, picked up her nail file and pointed to the Gare du Nord. 'You are here,' she said. 'And you want to go here. Do you see? So this is how you can get from one to the other.'

46

Two minutes later, Tim, Grk and Natascha were hurrying across the station, carrying the map. The woman in the tourist office had supplied them with strict instructions, explaining where to find the métro, how to buy tickets and which trains to take. Now they just had to get from the Gare du Nord to the Eiffel Tower before Max tried to kill Colonel Zinfandel.

Chapter 14

The woman in the tourist office had explained how to buy tickets. You got the best deal, she had said, if you bought a book of ten tickets rather than just one at a time.

Tim fed a twenty euro note into a ticket machine and pressed a button. Ten tickets spat out, followed by some change. He gave one ticket to Natascha, kept another in his hand and tucked the remaining eight into his pocket.

Natascha said, 'Do you think dogs need tickets?'

'They don't in London,' said Tim. 'So they probably don't here either.'

Grk wagged his tail. Although he didn't know what they were saying, he could tell that they were talking about him.

The three of them passed through the ticket barriers and hurried down the echoing corridors.

The woman in the tourist office had explained that there were two types of trains on the métro, the ordinary lines and the RER.

RER stands for *Réseau Express Régional*, which means Regional Express Network. RER trains are faster than ordinary métro trains. If Tim and Natascha wanted to get from the Gare du Nord to the Eiffel Tower as fast as possible, the woman had told them, they should definitely take the RER.

Following her instructions, they took an RER train heading south, changed at St Michel and went three more stops heading west.

Tim and Natascha sat side by side. Grk lay on the floor at their feet.

Natascha unfolded the leaflet that they had been given by the woman in the tourist office and relayed interesting facts to Tim. 'The Eiffel Tower was built in 1889,' she said. 'It is named after its designer, Gustav Eiffel. When it was built, it was the tallest building in the world, but it isn't any more.'

'What is?' said Tim.

Natascha skimmed through the rest of the leaflet. 'I don't know,' she said. 'It doesn't say.'

'I'll have to look it up when we get home,' said Tim. 'Does it say anything about the Jules Verne Restaurant?'

'Not much. It's on the second floor, apparently. And it's one of the best restaurants in Paris. Hey, this is interesting. Two hundred million people have visited the Eiffel Tower since it was built. Six million people go there every year. Which makes it the most visited monument on the planet.'

'After today, it will be two hundred million and two,' said Tim. 'Plus one dog.'

The train was easing into a station. Tim pointed at a sign on the wall which read TOUR EIFFEL. He said, 'This is where we get off.'

Natascha glanced at her watch. 'It's half past twelve,' she said, folding the leaflet and tucking it into her pocket. 'I hope we're not too late.'

49

Tim didn't answer. There was nothing to say. He knew what she meant. If they were too late, Max would be dead. When they got to the Tower, they would simply see his body lying on the floor, surrounded by the police and Colonel Zinfandel's bodyguards.

They just had to hope that they were in time to save him.

The doors slid open. Passengers poured out of the train and hurried along the platform. Natascha sprinted ahead of the crowd, determined not to waste another second. Tim and Grk hurried behind, trying to keep up with her. Tim knew that if he lost her among all these people, he would never be able to find her again.

They clambered up a flight of stairs and emerged into the street. There were trees on one side and a low wall on the other, separating the road from the river.

Tim looked around, but he couldn't see the Eiffel Tower. He felt confused. This was the right station. Even he could work out that *Tour Eiffel* was French for 'Eiffel Tower'. So where was the tower?

Natascha didn't bother looking or worrying. She just went straight to the nearest person who happened to be walking past, a tall, slim businessman in a smart, dark suit. He was carrying a leather briefcase in one hand and a fresh baguette in the other. Natascha said, '*Excusez-moi, monsieur. Où est la Tour Eiffel?*'

The businessman smiled, charmed by the little girl who asked directions so politely in such well-accented French. He turned round, raised his baguette and pointed. '*Voilà!*'

At the end of the outstretched baguette, there was the familiar shape of the Eiffel Tower.

When the businessman turned back again, his face dropped. The little girl had vanished. She might have spoken French with a good accent, but she hadn't bothered saying 'merci'. He looked up and down the street, wondering where she had gone.

There! There she was! Running away from him so fast that he wondered whether she might have stolen something. He checked his pockets, making sure that he still had his wallet and his keys.

Racing after her were a small boy and an even smaller dog. They were heading at full speed towards the Eiffel Tower.

The businessman stared after them, wondering who they were and what they were doing.

Chapter 15

Natascha wasn't an athlete. She didn't like sports. Given the choice between football, tennis, hockey and reading, she would always choose to stay at home with a good book. But today she ran so fast that she would have been guaranteed a place in the school athletics team.

She sped down the pavement, darted across the road and sprinted towards the Eiffel Tower. Cars swerved to avoid her. Brakes screeched. Angry drivers jammed their hands on their horns and yelled at the tops of their voices. Natascha took no notice. She didn't give a moment's thought to her own safety. All she cared about was finding Max.

Tim sprinted behind her, desperately trying to keep up. More cars swerved. More brakes screeched. More angry drivers yelled and hooted. Some of them even leaned out of their windows and shook their fists. Tim wished he could have stopped and apologised. He didn't like annoying anyone. But there was no time to waste. If he paused for a second, he would lose sight of Natascha and she would be gone forever.

Grk would have liked to stop too. He could smell warm fresh bread and fried onions and raw meat and all kinds of interesting smells which he would have liked to investigate. But he was attached to Tim's hand by a short leather lead, so he didn't have any choice about where he went. His little legs pattered on the pavement as he scrambled to keep up.

They ran through the lines of trees.

Ahead of them, the Eiffel Tower's great grey silhouette grew larger and taller until it appeared to be dominating the entire sky.

Tall buildings are usually surrounded by other tall buildings. If you go into the centre of most cities, for instance, several skyscrapers will be crowded together, making each of them look a little smaller and less impressive than it would alone.

The Eiffel Tower is different. There are no other buildings nearby, just trees and grass and flowerbeds. That is why the tallest building in Paris looks as if it might be the tallest building in the whole world. As Tim and Natascha ran through the park and came closer to the tower, they started to feel very, very small.

Grk didn't even notice the tower. He had seen several other dogs playing in the grass. They were sniffing the trees and the flowerbeds and one another. That looked fun! That was what he wanted to do too! Why couldn't he stop and sniff? But the leather lead took no notice of his wishes and dragged him onwards at full speed.

Tim and Natascha sprinted down a tarmac path, pulling Grk behind them, and arrived at the base of the Eiffel Tower. For a moment, they were both speechless. They looked around in amazement, stunned by the size of the structure above them. And then they remembered why they were here. Not to be amazed. Not to see the sights. But to find the Jules Verne Restaurant and rescue Max.

They searched for any sign of something which might look like a restaurant.

Above them, they could see the tower's extraordinary structure. It resembled a spider's web woven out of metal. Four huge legs came out of the sky and plunged into the earth, supporting the tower's vast mass.

There were lifts in the legs, taking tourists to the top of the Tower. People were standing patiently in long queues, waiting to go up in the lifts.

Hundreds of tourists were taking photos, angling their cameras at the tower, capturing the same views again and again.

Hawkers were selling little silver models of the Eiffel Tower to hang on your key ring and bigger bronze models to put on your mantelpiece.

Tim could see a crowd of people holding banners. There were words written on the banners. He strained his eyes, trying to read the letters. When he deciphered one of the banners, he tugged Natascha's sleeve. 'Look,' he said. 'That must be the place.'

Natascha turned round. As soon as she saw what he was pointing at, she said, 'Brilliant! That's it! Let's go.'

They pushed through the crowds.

Chapter 16

The Jules Verne Restaurant is one of the best restaurants in Paris. Lunch costs more than most people earn in a week. But it is still full almost every day. Diners are happy to pay a lot if the food is good enough. The view is good too. If you get a table by the window, you can look across the entire city.

The restaurant occupies a fantastic site on the second floor of the Eiffel Tower. A private lift takes diners up to the restaurant, then brings them down to the ground again at the end of their meal.

Today, a hundred people had assembled outside the entrance to the restaurant. Half were protestors and half were police.

The protestors were waving home-made banners with slogans painted in several different languages. Tim could read some, but others meant nothing to him.

DICTATORS NOT WELCOME IN PARIS! said one of the banners.

WE WANT OUR COUNTRY BACK!
RENTRE CHEZ TOI ZINFANDEL!
GEH NEZ HAUSE!

The protestors were Stanislavians who had escaped or been exiled from their own country when Colonel Zinfandel took power. Now they lived in France.

The protestors were surrounded by a ring of police,

who were preventing them from blocking the entrance to one of the smartest and most expensive restaurants in Paris.

Political protests are permitted in France. You can stand on the street and wave a banner, showing your disapproval of anyone or anything. But you are strictly forbidden from blocking the entrance to a restaurant. No one comes between the French and their food.

Natascha stood there for a moment, looking at the protestors and the restaurant, deciding where to go.

Tim and Grk stood beside her, waiting for her to make her decision.

Natascha was a proud Stanislavian. She loved her country. She was proud of her fellow Stanislavians who had come here to protest against Colonel Zinfandel. She would have liked to go and stand beside them to show her support. But she knew what would happen if she did. The police wouldn't allow her to go anywhere near the restaurant and she wouldn't have a chance to save her brother.

Tearing her eyes away from the protestors, Natascha hurried towards the entrance to the Jules Verne Restaurant.

Tim and Grk ran after her.

A man in a black uniform was standing beside the door marked 'Le Jules Verne'.

His name was Pierre Flaubert. He was the doorman.

He arrived at twelve o'clock in the morning and took up his position by the door. He stood there all afternoon

56

and all evening. He left at twelve o'clock at night. He welcomed diners to the restaurant, escorted them through the door and took them to the private lift.

Today, Pierre Flaubert ignored the protestors and the police. He didn't mind them. He was used to distractions. Every day, he was pestered by tourists, demanding to know whether they could go and eat in 'Le Jules Verne'. He always answered them in the same way. He produced a copy of the menu and thrust it into their hands.

'Have a look at this,' he would say. 'Choose what you like to eat.'

The tourists usually went away when they saw the prices.

When Pierre saw two children and a dog coming towards him, he didn't reach for a menu. He was sure they wouldn't ask for a reservation at the restaurant. They were probably looking for the toilets, he thought, or wanted to find a bowl of water for their dog. He smiled at them and said, '*Bonjour*.'

'*Bonjour*,' said Natascha. 'Do you speak English?'

'A little,' said Pierre. 'How can I help you?'

'We want to go the Jules Verne Restaurant. Can we go up in your lift?'

'Do you have a reservation?'

'No,' admitted Natascha. 'But we'd still like to go there.'

'Many people would like to go to Le Jules Verne,' said Pierre. 'But only those with reservations can use the lift.'

Tim said, 'Can't we go in the lift anyway?'

Pierre smiled and shook his head. 'I'm sorry, no, this is not possible. The lift is strictly reserved for people who are eating in the restaurant. Ordinary visitors must use the ordinary lift.'

'But there's a huge queue to go in the other lifts,' said Natascha. 'And we're in a hurry.'

Her words had no effect. Pierre simply shook his head. 'It is not permitted, *mademoiselle*. Not unless you have a reservation.'

Natascha said, 'Is Colonel Zinfandel having lunch there now?'

Pierre glanced at the crowd of protestors, then looked back at Natascha. Now he understood who she was. She had been sent to trap him. The protestors must be using her as a decoy, hoping he would be fooled by her innocent face into revealing some useful information. Well, he wasn't that stupid. He wouldn't be fooled by anyone.

'I am very sorry, *mademoiselle*,' said Pierre in a stern voice. 'I am not permitted to reveal the identities of our guests.'

His cold smile showed that the conversation was over. He crossed his arms and looked past Tim and Natascha as if they simply didn't exist.

When someone treats you like that, there are only two things that you can do. You can tread on their toe. Or you can pretend that they don't exist either. Natascha wasn't in a toe-treading mood, so she turned to Tim and, talking to him as if there was no one else within earshot,

58

she said, 'What are we going to do?'

'I don't know,' said Tim. 'What do you think?'

Natascha glanced at her watch. 'It's five to one. If we stand in those queues, we're going to have to wait for hours. We're never going to get to the restaurant in time.'

'Maybe Max isn't here either,' said Tim. 'Or maybe he's still waiting in one of the queues.'

Natascha tipped her head back and looked directly upwards. 'He's here,' she said.

'How do you know?' said Tim.

'I just do,' said Natascha. 'I can feel it. He's up there in the restaurant. And so is Colonel Zinfandel.'

She turned her head from side to side, looking at the enormous queues of people waiting for the lifts.

'We've got to get up there before they kill one another,' she said. 'And we don't have time to waste standing in one of those queues. So what are we going to do?'

Chapter 17

The Eiffel Tower is a thousand feet tall.

If you want to be precise, it is actually one thousand and sixty-three feet tall. And if you want to be metric, as the French always do, it is three hundred and twenty-four metres tall.

When the Eiffel Tower was built, it was the tallest building on the planet. That was in 1889. Since then, a whole stack of taller buildings have been built in different countries around the world. But the Eiffel Tower is still the tallest building in Paris, so you can see it from just about anywhere in the city.

It stands on four enormous feet, which were planted in the city's soil more than a hundred years ago and have stood there solidly since. The tower has survived wind, rain, thunder, lightning and two world wars.

Lifts and staircases lead from the ground to the first floor, which has a café and a viewing platform for looking over the city. The lifts continue to the second floor, which has a restaurant and another viewing platform. From there, you catch a different, smaller lift to the third floor, which has the best views of all.

Every year, several million people visit the Eiffel Tower. They go up in the lifts and look at the view over Paris. They want to see the views from the first floor, the second floor and the third floor.

It takes a long time for all these people to board the small lifts. So the queues are very long. People wait patiently. They know that everyone has to do the same thing. Rich or poor, tall or short, fat or thin, old or young, it doesn't matter. Whoever you are, if you want to go to the top of the tower, you have to wait in the queue.

Everyone is equal.

Everyone except two children and a small dog.

They were forcing their way to the front of the queue, pushing past people who had been waiting patiently for hours.

The girl was crying. The boy was mopping his eyes. Even the dog looked depressed. He stumbled along the ground with his head bowed, barely making the effort to sniff other people's ankles or poke his nose at their ice creams.

'Excuse me,' said the one of children as they passed down the queue. 'Sorry, can we get past? Thank you very much.'

'*Excusez-moi de vous déranger*,' said the other child. '*Je suis desolée. Pardon, pardon. Merci beaucoup.*'

Most people were too polite to stop the children. Hardly anyone demanded to know why they were jumping the queue or asked why they couldn't wait like everyone else. But if anyone did ask any questions, the boy simply wept even louder and the dog howled and the girl said in a pitiful voice, 'We're lost! *Nous sommes perdus!* Our parents have gone up the tower without us! *Nos parents ont disparus dans la tour!* We've got to go and find them!'

She never needed to say anything else. No one could be cruel enough to keep two lost children from their parents. People stepped aside and ushered Natascha, Tim and Grk towards the front of the queue. 'These poor children have lost their parents,' said one of the tourists. 'Let them past,' said another. 'Lost kids coming through!' yelled a third. Up and down the queue, people discussed what had happened to the children and asked if they needed any help.

Natascha felt guilty. And so did Tim. They didn't like what they were doing. But they didn't have much choice.

It's never polite to jump a queue. When other people have been waiting longer than you, it's only fair that they should go first.

But when you're trying to save your brother from certain death, you don't have time to worry about being polite.

They soon arrived at the front of the queue, where three cashiers were sitting behind a long desk. Tim handed over a twenty-euro note. The cashier handed back two tickets and some change.

'*Merci*,' said Tim. He gave one ticket to Natascha and kept the other for himself.

'*Bonne chance*,' said the cashier, who had already heard what everyone else was saying. 'Good luck. I hope you find your mother and your father.'

'*Merci beaucoup*,' said Natasha and hurried into the Eiffel Tower.

'Thank you,' added Tim. '*Merci beaucoup*.' He stood

there awkwardly for a moment, feeling guilty that he had told such an outrageous lie. Then he reminded himself not to be so foolish. There was nothing wrong with telling a little lie if it saved Max's life. He thanked the cashier again and hurried after Natascha.

Tim, Grk and Natascha went through the turnstiles, ran up some stairs and boarded a lift. It was already packed with people, who shuffled backwards, making some space so the two children and their dog could squeeze inside.

The doors slid shut. The lift juddered, then started moving slowly upwards, easing up the edge of the Eiffel Tower like an ant crawling up a man's leg.

Tim and Natascha stayed in the lift until it reached the second floor. There, the doors slid open and the passengers poured out.

The lift operator was wearing a yellow uniform. Natascha went up to him and said, '*Excusez-moi, monsieur. Où est le* Jules Verne?'

'*Le* Jules Verne?' said the lift operator. '*Il est là.*'

'*Merci beaucoup*,' said Natascha and hurried in the direction that he had pointed. Tim and Grk ran after her. They went down a corridor and soon came to a door. It was guarded by a man in a black uniform.

'We've come to meet our parents,' said Natascha, assuming that the guard would speak English. 'They're having lunch inside. Can you let us in, please?'

'Of course,' said the guard. He had no reason to disbelieve what she was saying. Parents often brought their children to the Eiffel Tower. The guard opened the door and ushered them into the restaurant.

Natascha went first. Tim and Grk followed.

The door closed behind them.

The Jules Verne was calm and quiet and peaceful.

People were concentrating all their attention on the serious business of eating very expensive food.

They put tiny morsels in their mouths and mopped their lips with thick white napkins. Waiters in black suits glided between the tables, carrying plates and bottles. The only sounds were the clinking of cutlery and the murmur of polite conversation.

And there was one other sound too, even quieter than the clinking or the murmurs.

It was the sound of a gasp.

The gasp came from Natascha.

Her hand flew to her mouth. Her face went white. She had seen, sitting on the far side of the restaurant, the man who had murdered her parents.

Chapter 18

A tall, thin waiter stood at the front of the restaurant. He was wearing a black uniform and gold-rimmed glasses. He welcomed diners when they arrived at the restaurant, showed them to their tables and ensured that every moment of their meal was memorable.

When he saw two children and a dog coming through the door, he stared at them for a moment, wondering what on earth they were doing in his restaurant. He didn't like children and he didn't like dogs. Given the choice, he would have preferred to ban them from the restaurant entirely. But some misguided parents insisted on bringing their children when they came to eat at the Jules Verne. And other even more misguided people brought their dogs. These three intruders must be the children and the pet of someone who was eating here.

The waiter stepped forward, looked down his long nose at the children and the dog, and said, 'Oui? Puis-je vous aider?'

Neither Natascha nor Tim said a word. Tim hadn't understood what the waiter had said and Natascha hadn't even heard him. All her attention was focused on a long table at the other side of the room.

Natascha couldn't see Colonel Zinfandel's face, but she recognised him by the shape of his head and shoulders. He was sitting at the near end of the table with his back to the door. He was throwing back his head and laughing loudly at something that someone had said.

Down on the ground, Grk growled. The bristles stood up on the back of his neck. He had seen Colonel Zinfandel too. Even more importantly, he had smelt him. And the smell filled Grk with fury.

The waiter was getting impatient. He clasped his hands together, peered through his glasses at the children and said in a low voice, '*Vos parents sont ici?*'

Tim looked at the Natascha, then the waiter, and realised he would have to say something. So he said, 'I don't speak French.'

'Then you are lucky,' said the waiter in a strong French accent. 'Because I speak English. So, tell me. Are your parents here?'

Tim stared stupidly at the waiter, wondering what to say.

'You have come to meet your parents?' said the waiter. 'What are their names? Where are they?'

Tim stayed silent.

'Can you see them?' said the waiter, who was starting to lose patience. 'Please, point them out to me.'

'They're not here,' said Tim, suddenly feeling awkward and ashamed.

Now the waiter understood what was happening. These children were ordinary tourists who had wandered in here by mistake, somehow slipping past the guard on the door, and now they were determined to cause chaos in his beautiful restaurant. When he spoke again, his voice

66

was stronger and more insistent. 'You must leave now. Come on, children. It is time for you to go.'

The waiter's voice snapped Natascha's attention away from Colonel Zinfandel and back to her present situation. She took a deep breath and tried to forget that she was standing in the same room as the man who had murdered her parents. Then she turned to the waiter, gave him a radiant smile and said in a calm voice, 'We would like a table for two, please.'

The waiter stared at her. 'A table?'

'That's right,' said Natasha. 'For two.'

'You wish to eat?'

'Yes,' said Natascha. 'This is a restaurant, isn't it?'

'But you are a child!'

'I still like eating,' said Natascha. 'And I'm very hungry. So can we have a table for two, please?'

The waiter looked down his long nose at her. 'If you want to eat, *mademoiselle*, there is another restaurant on the first level of the Tower which will be more suitable for you. If you go there, you will be able to buy yourself a burger and some chips.'

'We don't want a burger and chips,' said Natascha. 'We want to eat in this restaurant.' She pointed at a nearby table which had been set for two. 'Can we sit at this table, please?'

The waiter stared at her. He was speechless. He had been working as a waiter for fifteen years, but he had never been presented with a situation like this. Two children had walked into his restaurant and demanded to be treated like adults.

The waiter didn't have a clue what to do. He knew very little about children, but he would have guessed that these ones were only ten or eleven years old. What were they doing in his restaurant? And now they were here, what was he supposed to do with them?

After a moment's thought, he realised who these children were. They must be the son and daughter of a multi-millionaire. Or, even worse, they were the offspring of important, influential politicians. Who else would have the cheek to come in here and demand a table? If he threw them out of the restaurant, their parents would march into the restaurant, summon the manager and make sure he was fired. There was only one thing that he could do. He smiled at Natascha and said, 'Of course, *mademoiselle*. We should be pleased to serve lunch for you both. Please, come and sit down.'

'Thank you,' said Natascha.

The waiter led Tim and Natascha to the table. They sat down. Grk crawled under the table and lay at their feet. The waiter unfurled two thick white napkins, placed one on each of their laps and went to fetch some menus.

When the waiter had gone, Tim stared at Natascha and whispered, 'What are we going to do now?'

'Have lunch,' said Natascha. 'I'm hungry. Aren't you?'

'Yes. But ... '

'But what?'

'This is the poshest restaurant I've ever been in.'

'Me too,' said Natascha. She looked around the restaurant and smiled confidently as if she ate in places like this every day of the week. 'It's nice, isn't it?'

'But...'

Natascha fixed Tim with a strong stare. 'Can you stop saying "but" like that? It's really quite annoying.'

'Sorry. But...'

'You're doing it again. Just don't.'

'Sorry.'

'Look, Tim, it's very simple. Colonel Zinfandel is here. Max isn't. Not yet, anyway. He will be soon. And I want to be here when he arrives. So can you just relax and enjoy having lunch in the one of the best restaurants in Paris?'

'I suppose so,' said Tim.

He couldn't say anything else because the waiter had returned with three leather-bound menus. He handed one menu to each of the children, then offered the third to Tim. 'Will you have the wine list, *monsieur*?'

'No, thanks,' said Tim. 'I don't drink wine.'

The waiter looked at Natascha. 'For you, *mademoiselle*? A glass of wine? Or some champagne?'

'Not today, thank you,' said Natascha. 'I'd like an orange juice.'

'Me too,' said Tim.

'*Deux jus d'orange*,' said the waiter with a thin-lipped smile. He turned on his heel and walked away, leaving Tim and Natascha to read their menus.

Chapter 19

Scallops, medallion, truffle, langoustine, turbot, zabaglione.

Tim stared at these words, wondering what they meant.

He supposed they must be food. Otherwise they wouldn't be on a menu in a restaurant. But what type of food? Which one should he pick for lunch? And when it arrived, would he actually want to eat it?

He glanced at Natascha, hoping she would be looking as confused as he felt, but she was reading her menu with obvious pleasure, imagining all the different delicious dishes that she could choose to eat.

Tim sighed and started reading again from the top.

The menus were written in both French and English, so Tim could understand the actual words that were written on them, but that didn't really help him. What was a langoustine? And what were you supposed to do with a medallion?

Tim sighed again. He looked at Natascha and said, 'What are you going to have?'

'I haven't quite decided,' said Natascha. 'But I'll probably have the scallops followed by the turbot. What about you?'

'I'll have whatever you're having,' said Tim. He shut his menu and looked around the restaurant.

It was built into the structure of the Eiffel Tower. Through the windows, Tim could see the Tower's steel struts. Beyond them, the whole city was spread out like a map. He could see tiny cars and buses driving through the streets and miniature boats sailing along the river.

He wondered how far up they were. He tried to imagine what would happen if someone fell out of the window. They would topple through the air, turning over and over and over, then land on the ground with a loud splat.

The waiter returned with two tall glasses of orange juice. He placed them on the table and said, 'Are you ready to order?'

'Yes, we are,' said Natasha. 'I would like to start with the scallops. And then I'll have the turbot.'

The waiter nodded politely, then turned to Tim. 'And for you, sir?'

'I'll have the same as her,' said Tim.

'A very good choice, sir.' The waiter scrawled their order in a small pad. He had decided to pretend that Tim and Natascha were just ordinary customers and their age was nothing unusual. He would treat them as graciously as he would anyone else.

When the waiter had gone, Tim sipped his orange juice. It was delicious. He said, 'What are scallops?'

'A type of shellfish,' said Natascha. 'Like oysters or mussels.'

'Oh,' said Tim. He didn't think he liked oysters or mussels, so he was fairly sure he wouldn't like scallops either. 'And what's turbot?'

'It's a fish too.'

'Okay,' said Tim. He had suddenly remembered the waiter recommending the restaurant on the Tower's lower level. 'You will be able to buy a burger and some chips,' the waiter had said. Mmmm, thought Tim. Burger and chips. That sounded good.

Tim suddenly realised he was really quite hungry. He started to dream about a squishy burger covered in ketchup and surrounded by chips. He was just imagining exactly how the chips would taste when a voice broke his concentration.

The voice belonged to Natascha. She whispered in an urgent tone: 'Look!'

Tim lifted his head and looked at her. 'Hmmm?'

'I said look!'

'What am I supposed to be looking at?'

Natascha didn't move. Her face was rigid. She whispered, 'That.'

Tim turned his head to see what she was staring at.

On the other side of the restaurant, a boy was walking across the dining room, heading straight towards Colonel Zinfandel. It was Max.

Tim whispered, 'What's he going to do?'

Natascha didn't answer. She couldn't speak. She was desperately trying to decide what to do. Should she run forward and stop Max? Or should she let him come into the restaurant and kill the man who had murdered their parents? Indecision rooted her to the spot.

With each moment that she hesitated, Max took another step into the room. And each step brought him closer to Colonel Zinfandel.

Tim didn't know what to do either. He was Max's friend. And Natascha's too. He knew how much they hated Colonel Zinfandel and he understood why. But should he simply sit still and watch a man get murdered?

He didn't know whether to run or shout or throw himself forward or simply sit still and keep quiet and let Max do what he wanted.

Under the table, Grk was standing up. His ears were upright. His mouth was open. His tongue was hanging out. He had seen Max.

Grk was confused. Max was here. And Colonel Zinfandel too. What was going on?

He looked up at Tim and Natascha, wondering why they hadn't moved. Why weren't they running across the restaurant to say hello? That was what Grk wanted to do. But he knew he shouldn't. Not if Tim and Natascha weren't. So he stood there, his tail wagging and his mouth open, waiting to see what they did.

When Max reached Colonel Zinfandel, he stopped. And looked around. He was searching for a weapon.

On a nearby table, he saw a knife.

Max grabbed it.

He gripped the wooden handle in his right hand. The sharp blade gleamed in the bright lights. He said, 'Zinfandel.'

Colonel Zinfandel didn't turn round. He was immersed in his conversation and didn't want to be disturbed.

Max spoke again, louder this time. His voice was strong and clear. He said, 'Zinfandel.'

73

This time, Colonel Zinfandel turned round to see who had interrupted him. His brows were furrowed and his mouth was open. He stared at Max and said, 'Yes? Who are you?'

'You don't know me?'

'I've never seen you before,' said Colonel Zinfandel. 'How should I know you?'

'You have seen me before. My name is Max Raffifi.'

'Raffifi? I once knew a man named Raffifi. His name was Gabriel Raffifi.'

'That was my father.'

Colonel Zinfandel smiled. 'So, you're the son of Gabriel Raffifi. And what do you want me with me?'

'To kill you,' said Max. 'Just like you killed my father.'

'Your father was a fool,' said Colonel Zinfandel. 'And I can see that you are too.'

That was enough for Max. He didn't need to say another word. He knew what he had to do. In a single, swift, sudden movement, he pointed the knife at Colonel Zinfandel's heart and hurled himself forwards.

A loud shriek pierced the air.

'No!'

Max recognised his sister's voice.

He paused. Only for a moment. But that was enough.

Colonel Zinfandel jabbed with his right fist and knocked the knife from Max's hand. The blade spun through the air and clattered to the floor.

There was a moment of stillness.

No one moved and no one spoke.

And then everyone moved at once. Colonel Zinfandel's bodyguards reached for their weapons. Some diners screamed. Others shouted. And Max ran.

Max was brave, but he wasn't a fool. He knew he wasn't any match for Colonel Zinfandel and his bodyguards. He sprinted towards his sister, grabbed her by the shoulder and, pulling her after him, charged towards the door.

Tim sprang out of his chair and went after them.

Grk ran too. He didn't know what was happening, but if Tim and Natascha and Max were running, he wanted to run with them.

A waiter was standing in the middle of the restaurant, carrying two plates on a silver tray. There was a baked fish on one plate and a hot steak on the other.

Tim darted one way round the waiter.

Natascha went the other.

The waiter swerved, trying to avoid them. His arm dipped. The tray tipped over. Plates went flying. The steak soared through the air. The fish flipped and flapped as if it was still alive. And then with a

SQUELCH!

and a

SPLAT!

the steak landed on the floor, swiftly followed by the fish.

Grk whirled round and stared at the thick, juicy steak. Then he turned his head and stared at Tim, Natascha and Max. They had reached the door and were just about to leave the restaurant.

Grk wavered. He didn't know what to do.

There was nothing that he liked more than steak. The scent filled his nostrils. It would only take a moment to nip back into the restaurant and grab it in his mouth and sink his teeth into that warm delicious meat and ...

'Grk!'

Natascha yelled at him from the doorway.

Grk tore his eyes away from the steak and galloped to join the others.

Before anyone had a chance to grab them or stop them or trip them up or even realise what was really happening, they reached the door and ran out of the restaurant.

The door swung shut behind them.

Chapter 20

If you spend a large sum of money when you visit a restaurant, you are entitled to expect certain things. Superb food, of course. And fine wine. And discreet, attentive service.

But you would not expect to see a boy attacking a man with a knife.

None of the diners in the restaurant knew what to do. Nothing like this had ever happened to them before. Were they watching a show? Or a scene from a movie? They sat in their chairs, blinking and staring, wondering what was going on.

The waiters were just as shocked as the diners. They stood still, their mouths open and their brains whirring, trying to make sense of what had just happened.

Only one person reacted quickly. That was Colonel Zinfandel. He turned to his bodyguards and snarled at them in a low, angry voice. 'What are you doing?'

The bodyguards stared stupidly at him as if they couldn't understand what he was saying.

'What are you waiting for?' said Colonel Zinfandel.

Still none of them answered. None of them dared speak.

'Are you just going to stand there like idiots?' said Colonel Zinfandel. 'Or are you going to stop them?'

His six bodyguards didn't even attempt to answer any

of these questions. When you are a bodyguard, you know that actions speak louder than words. They pushed back their chairs and sprinted towards the door, chasing after the three children and the dog.

Colonel Zinfandel turned to his fellow diners. He was a handsome man. When he smiled, his white teeth gleamed under the bright lights. 'I am very sorry,' he said in a calm voice. 'I appear to have been the victim of an assassination attempt. I hope it hasn't spoiled your lunch.'

Colonel Zinfandel was cruel and vicious and brutal, but he could also be very charming when he chose to be.

'We're absolutely fine,' said one of the other men at the table.

'Of course we're fine,' said another. 'No one tried to kill us.'

'But what about you?' said a third. 'Are you hurt? Do you need to see a doctor? Shouldn't we call an ambulance?'

'No, no, there's no need,' said Colonel Zinfandel, shrugging his shoulders. 'I'm used to events like this. I come from a complicated country, you see. Stanislavia is not like France or England or the United States of America. In my country, people don't settle their arguments with words. They use fists and guns. So I know how to defend myself.' He smiled again. His white teeth seemed to gleam even more brightly. 'Now, if you'll excuse me, I'm going to go and see whether my men have caught those assassins. I would very much like to know who they are.'

78

Some of his fellow diners wondered whether they should call the police. Others offered to accompany him.

'Thank you so much,' said Colonel Zinfandel. 'But there's no need for you to interrupt your meal. My men are sure to have everything under control. I will be back in a moment. While I'm gone, please just enjoy the food and the wine and the view.'

With another dazzling smile, Colonel Zinfandel turned his back on the table and marched towards the door.

As soon as his back was turned, his smile vanished.

It was replaced by an expression of intense anger.

Colonel Zinfandel was boiling with rage.

He had been made to look like a fool.

Before his limousine even arrived at the Eiffel Tower, his bodyguards had surrounded the Jules Verne Restaurant. His men had been watching every entrance and exit. They had been given strict orders about exactly what to do. No one should have been allowed inside without proper authorisation.

The restaurant should have been the safest place in the whole of Paris. But a child had slipped past the bodyguards and got inside.

Three children, in fact. And a dog.

And not just any children. The son and daughter of Gabriel Raffifi. And that English boy, the one called Tim, who had helped them escape from prison.

Now they had come back to haunt him.

They had attacked him. They had sneaked up behind him and tried to kill him. They had come this close to burying a knife in his heart. He had been too quick and too clever for them, of course. But they had still managed to escape.

It doesn't matter, thought Colonel Zinfandel. I'm going to catch them now.

And when I've caught them, I will make them suffer.

I will show them that no one makes a fool of Colonel Zinfandel.

Chapter 21

Max came to a standstill in the middle of the second level of the Eiffel Tower. Natascha and Tim and Grk stopped beside him. They looked around, searching for any sign of Colonel Zinfandel. He hadn't got here yet. Nor had his bodyguards. But they would be soon.

Max looked at the others.

He knew that there wasn't any time to ask all the questions that he wanted to ask. What are you doing here? What are *you* doing here? How did you get here? How did you find me? How did you know where to go? And why couldn't you do as I asked and leave me alone? Those questions could wait. First, they had to escape from the broad-shouldered and heavily armed men who were chasing them.

'Up or down,' said Max. 'That's the question.'

Three large lifts bring large groups of tourists from the ground to the second level of the Eiffel Tower. Four more smaller lifts take smaller groups of tourists from the second level to the top. And when you reach the top, there is only one way to go: back down again to the bottom.

'Down,' said Tim. 'If we go up, we'll be trapped at the top.'

'Up,' said Natascha. 'They'll be expecting us to go down. They'll be waiting for us at the bottom. If we go up, we'll get away from them.'

Max looked around, wondering what to do, trying to decide whether to go up or down.

The decision was made for him. He could see Colonel Zinfandel's bodyguards fighting their way through the crowd, thrusting people aside and searching for any sign of three children and a dog. He could also see the long lines of tourists waiting for the lifts going down to the ground.

'This way,' said Max. 'Follow me. We're going to go up.'

He darted forwards and clambered over a low metal fence. The others hurried after him. They went down a corridor and found themselves beside the small lifts that took tourists to the top of the Tower. A sign said:

VERS LE SOMMET
TO THE TOP

A door was closing. Max lunged forwards and planted himself in the way, holding the door for the others.

Inside the lift people protested, demanding to know what he thought he was doing. Max ignored them. He held the door open until Tim and Natascha and Grk had stepped inside the lift. Then Max stepped inside himself and the door slid shut. People shuffled backwards, making room for the three children. Grk squatted at their feet, watching out for other people's legs. He didn't want to be trodden on again.

The lift was ready to leave. The bodyguards wouldn't get into this one. But they would be coming in the next one. They would only be a few moments behind.

The lift shuddered upwards towards the summit.

Tim stared out of the window at the view. He could see the Tower's metal struts and, beyond them, the river and the city. Hundreds of metres below, boats cruised slowly along the glistening water. Tiny cars whizzed along the roads. Tim wished he was down there now, rather than up here, locked in a small lift.

Max turned to his sister. It was his first chance to talk to her. Other people could hear him, but he was so angry that he didn't care about their presence. He said, 'What are you doing here? How did you find me? Why did you stop me? Are you crazy?'

Natascha didn't know which one of these questions to answer, so she didn't answer any of them. She just said, 'Are you okay?'

'No,' said Max. 'I'm not okay at all. I was this close.' He placed his fingers together, leaving a tiny gap between them. 'This close! And you stopped me. Why did you do that?'

'I wanted to help you,' said Natascha.

'Help me?' Max shook his head. 'What's wrong with you? Don't you know who he is? Don't you know what he did to our parents?'

'Of course I do,' said Natascha.

'Then why did you stop me?'

'Because killing people is wrong.'

Max laughed bitterly. 'Tell that to Colonel Zinfandel.'

'If you kill him, then you're as bad as he is.'

'Evil deeds should be punished,' said Max. 'Don't you understand that? Don't you understand anything?'

Max and Natascha were just about to start shouting at one another when Tim interrupted both of them. 'Why don't you finish this argument later?' he said. 'Right now, we've got more important things to worry about. Like how to get away from those guards. And how to stay alive.'

Natascha and Max looked at Tim. They knew he was right. If they didn't think of a way to escape, Colonel Zinfandel would kill them himself and their arguments would be completely pointless.

At that moment, the lift stopped and the door opened. They had arrived on the top of the Eiffel Tower. Max stepped out of the lift, followed by the others. They looked at their surroundings.

They were standing on the top of the tallest building in Paris. From here, they could see the whole city. A strong metal fence protected them from the empty air. Even if you were crazy enough to want to throw yourself off, you couldn't. There was no way anyone could squeeze themselves through that fence. Not even Grk was small enough to get through the holes.

Tourists were lingering by the balcony, taking photos of the view or looking through one of the solid metal telescopes which watched over Paris.

Tim, Max and Natascha stared at the fence, the view and the long drop to the ground.

'This is hopeless,' said Natascha. 'We can't run. We can't hide. There's nowhere to go. What are we going to do?'

'I've got an idea,' said Tim.

The others turned to look at him.

Tim pointed at Natascha's rucksack. 'Open your bag.'

Chapter 22

The lift stopped on the top floor of the Eiffel Tower. The door opened. Colonel Zinfandel walked out, followed by four bodyguards.

They were wearing black suits, white shirts and black ties.

If you had seen them in the street, you might have imagined that they were ordinary businessmen, hurrying towards a meeting. But if you got into a fight with them, you would know immediately that there was nothing ordinary about these men. They were highly trained killers.

The four bodyguards appeared to be unarmed, but appearances can be deceptive. Each of them was actually carrying a Glock 19 pistol in a leather holster under his left arm.

As you probably know, the Glock 19 is the ideal weapon for bodyguards. It is small enough that it can be worn in a concealed holster, but big enough to do some serious damage to an opponent.

In a curt tone, Colonel Zinfandel delivered his orders to the four bodyguards. They divided into two groups. Two went to the left. The other two followed Colonel Zinfandel to the right. They walked briskly, looking around, searching for the assassins.

The terrace was packed with tourists, who were

standing by the balcony, staring at the amazing views over Paris. Some were taking photos. Others were peering through binoculars and telescopes.

Colonel Zinfandel and his soldiers glanced quickly at each of the tourists. They knew exactly what they were looking for. Three children and a dog. They weren't interested in anyone else. Which was why they took no notice of a fat man standing by the balcony.

He was staring at the view, so they could only see his back, but they didn't bother coming closer to look at his face. They were searching for children and dogs, not fat men.

If Colonel Zinfandel or his soldiers had bothered to stop and taken a longer look at the fat man, they wouldn't have been fooled so easily. They would have seen immediately that he had some strange kinks in his body. Then they would have noticed that he was wearing some extremely unusual clothes. He had a blanket draped around his shoulders, for instance. His shoes were unexpectedly small for a man with such a large body. And as for his face ... Well, if the soldiers had decided to come a little closer and peer at the fat man's face, they would have seen that he didn't look like a man at all.

But they just gave him a quick glance, nothing more, and then moved onwards, searching for children and dogs.

As soon as they had gone past, the fat man fell to pieces.

Chapter 23

The fat man's head dropped towards the floor. His back broke in half. His body became four bodies.

He wasn't really a fat man. He was actually a girl, two boys and a dog wrapped in a long brown blanket.

Natascha had been sitting on Max's shoulders. Tim and Grk had been crouching at his feet. They had taken the blanket from Natascha's rucksack and wrapped it around themselves.

Now they had to run.

Natascha reached for the blanket, but Max pulled her away.

'There isn't time,' he hissed. 'Leave it!'

Natascha dropped the blanket. She knew Max was right. They had a few seconds, nothing more. And then the four bodyguards would have walked round the entire terrace.

The bodyguards would realise they had been tricked. And they would come back to see who had tricked them.

It was better to lose a blanket than get caught by Colonel Zinfandel.

They ran towards the lifts, leaving the blanket sprawled on the ground. Max looked from side to side, checking they weren't being followed. He couldn't see any sign of the bodyguards, which meant that they must still be on the other side of the terrace.

One of the lifts was ready to leave. Max darted inside and held the door. The others followed him. As soon as they were safely inside, Max released the door and it slid shut. The lift started moving immediately.

'We're free,' said Natascha as the lift juddered downwards from the third level to the second. 'We're safe!'

'Not yet,' said Tim. 'They might have the Tower surrounded.'

'So what are we going to do?'

'We're going to run,' said Max. 'This lift stops on the second floor. We have to get a different lift from there to the ground. As soon as the lift stops and the door opens, we start running – and we don't stop running till we're in the other lift. Okay?'

The others nodded.

'We should each go in a different direction,' said Max. 'Then they might catch one of us, or even two, but not all three. As soon as the lift stops, I'll go to the left. Natascha, you go to the right. And Tim, you go straight ahead. Okay?'

Tim and Natascha nodded.

'Grk can come with me,' said Tim. He turned to Natascha. 'Unless you want to take him.'

Natascha shook her head. 'No, you take him. That's safer. You can run faster than me.' She knelt on the ground and tickled Grk's ears, then leaned forward, put her mouth close to his ear and whispered something to him so quietly that no one else could hear what she said.

Grk wagged his tail. He seemed to like whatever she'd said.

'We've got to arrange a rendezvous,' said Max.

'A what?' said Tim.

'A meeting place,' said Max. 'Any ideas?'

'Notre Dame,' said Natascha immediately.

'Perfect,' said Max. 'We'll meet inside. At the front. Opposite the altar.'

Natascha shook her head. 'What about Grk? He won't be allowed inside a church.'

'Then let's meet outside,' said Max. 'At the front entrance.'

'See you there,' said Natascha.

But Tim wasn't so sure. He said, 'What's Notre Dame?'

'It's a big church in the middle of Paris,' explained Natascha.

'How am I supposed to find it?' said Tim. 'I've never been here before.'

'Ask anyone,' said Max. 'Everyone in Paris knows Notre Dame. Just stop someone in the street and ask them to point you in the right direction.'

'But I can't speak French,' said Tim. 'What am I supposed to say?'

'Repeat after me,' said Natascha. '*Où est Notre Dame?*'

'*Où est Notre Dame?*' said Tim.

Natascha winced at his accent. 'Try again,' she said, speaking very slowly and pronouncing every syllable separately. '*Où est Notre Dame?*'

'*Où* ...' said Tim. But before he could say another word, the lift slowed down and stopped. There wasn't going to be time for him to practise his pronunciation. They had reached the second floor.

Max said, 'Ready?'

The others nodded.

'Ready,' said Natascha.

'Ready,' said Tim.

Grk wagged his tail. He knew they were playing a game. He wasn't exactly sure of the rules, but he didn't really mind. He liked games.

They tensed their muscles, preparing to run.

The door slid open. Max was the first to go. He stepped out of the lift, turned to the left and sprinted straight into the arms of a bodyguard.

Chapter 24

The bodyguard looked at the three children and smiled.

He was a big man with broad shoulders and strong muscles. He knew his own strength and he was sure that three children didn't have a hope of escaping from him. They would simply put their arms in the air and surrender. He opened his jacket, showing the pistol in the holster under his arm, then stepped forwards and placed his right hand on Max's shoulder.

'You'd better come with me,' said the bodyguard in a deep voice. 'Colonel Zinfandel is waiting for you.'

Max didn't answer. He just kicked the bodyguard between the legs.

'Oooooooff!' The bodyguard bent forwards, his face creased in agony.

Max pushed the bodyguard aside and ran past. He didn't look back at Tim or Natascha. He knew they could take care of themselves.

And he was right. Natascha was already running in the opposite direction. Tim stepped over the writhing bodyguard and sprinted to the end of the corridor. Grk ran alongside him.

Max had turned left, so Tim turned right. He hurried across the terrace, dodging round tourists, putting as much distance as possible between himself and the bodyguard, hoping he hadn't been followed.

He wondered what to do next.

He was running across the second level of the Eiffel Tower, hundreds of metres above the ground. There was only one way to escape from the men who were chasing him. He had to get off the Tower and onto the ground. Then he could disappear into the streets of Paris and shake off his pursuers.

How should he get down to the ground?

He had two options. He could take a lift or he could walk down the stairs. The lift would be quicker, but Tim preferred the thought of the stairs. He didn't like the prospect of finding himself trapped in a small space with Colonel Zinfandel or one of his bodyguards.

He looked around, searching for the stairs. There! He could see an entrance cut into the floor. He pushed through the crowd. Grk trotted alongside him. They reached the stairs and jogged down.

A moment later, they were alone on a skinny staircase descending towards the ground.

The stairs were enclosed by a fence. You couldn't get through or fall off. You could only go up or down.

Tim and Grk went down.

And down.

And down.

The only noise was the rattle of their footsteps against the metal stairs. Tappity-tappity-tappity-tappity-tap! Tappity-tappity-tappity-tappity-tap! Tappity-tappity-tappity-tappity-tap!

The stairs were mesmerising. Down and down and down and down and down. Step after step after step after step after step. They seemed to go on for ever.

Every minute or two, Tim and Grk passed other people coming up, holding the handrail and hauling themselves slowly from step to step. Going up was much more difficult than going down. You should have taken the lift, Tim wanted to say, but he didn't have any spare time to say anything. Nor did he have breath to waste. He just ran past, hoping he wasn't going to meet any of Colonel Zinfandel's bodyguards.

And he didn't. He must have outsmarted them by choosing the stairs rather than the lifts.

But if they were guarding the lifts, checking who got in and who got out, wouldn't they have caught Max and Natascha?

He couldn't worry about that. Not now. The others would have to take care of themselves. He just had to concentrate on saving himself. Later, when he reached Notre Dame, he could worry about the others.

The stairs went on and on.

Tappity-tappity-tappity-tappity-tap!

Step after step after step after step after step.

Tappity-tappity-tappity-tappity-tap!

Down and down and down and down and down.

Tappity-tappity-tappity-tappity-tap!

Just as Tim was beginning to think they would never reach the ground, he saw a doorway. It was the exit.

Tim was exhausted, but he still had a big grin on his face. He looked down at Grk and said, 'We've done it! We're free!'

Grk wagged his tail and gave a joyful bark.

GRRRFF!

Together, Tim and Grk jogged down the last few steps and emerged from the Eiffel Tower. They found themselves in the midst of a large crowd. They had walked straight into one of the queues of people waiting to go up in a lift.

Tim felt proud of himself. He had escaped. He was free. He had managed to outwit Colonel Zinfandel and his bodyguards. Now he just had to find his way to Notre Dame – and hope that Max and Natascha had managed to escape too. He looked at Grk. 'Can you remember what Natascha said I should say?'

This time, Grk didn't wag his tail. Nor did he bark. He didn't appear to have heard what Tim said.

'I think it was *"Où est Notre Dame?"'* said Tim. 'Is that right? *"Où est Notre Dame?"'*

Grk still didn't answer. All his attention was focused elsewhere. His ears were upright. His fur was standing on end. His tail was between his legs. He looked tense and alert.

'What is it?' said Tim. 'What's wrong?'

Grk lifted his head to look at Tim, then turned back again to look across the concrete.

Tim turned to see what Grk was looking at.

At first, he couldn't see anything unusual. There were long queues for the lifts. Tourists were taking photos. Dogs and toddlers were running around. People were selling little silver models of the Eiffel Tower. Everything looked normal. And then he noticed a broad-shouldered man pushing through the crowds, coming towards him.

It was the same bodyguard who had seen them coming out of the lift on the second floor. He must have recovered from Max's kick and come down to the ground to wait for them. Now he was only a few metres away.

For a second, Tim was too surprised to move. He stood there, staring stupidly at the bodyguard, allowing him to come even closer.

The bodyguard roared.

Who was he shouting at? And what was he saying?

Tim immediately saw the answers to his own questions. More men were coming towards him from every direction. They must have been waiting at the exits. Now they had been alerted by the bodyguard's shouts.

They were coming to get him.

Tim knew he didn't have a chance. He was just a small, thin boy. Protected by nothing except a small dog. He didn't have a gun. He couldn't fight. What could he do against a group of soldiers?

Shouldn't he just put his hands in the air and surrender?

He glanced at the ground.

Grk wagged his tail. His ears were upright. His jaws were open, showing his small white teeth. He was ready to defend himself.

Me too, thought Tim.

They weren't going to surrender. They weren't going to allow themselves to be captured. No, they were going to fight with every drop of their strength.

He jerked Grk's lead.

'Come on,' he yelled. 'Run!'

Grk didn't need any encouragement. He turned round and sprinted across the concrete, heading away from the tower and towards the river. Tim charged after him.

Behind them, Tim could hear more shouting. Not just one voice this time. Lots of voices. Ten or twenty men shouting to one another. He knew what that meant. The Stanislavian Secret Service were following him. They would be coming from every direction, hoping to cut him off and trap him and catch him and take him to Colonel Zinfandel. Well, he didn't want that to happen. He wanted to be free. He put his head down and ran as fast as he had ever run in his life.

Chapter 25

One ordinary boy against a troop of highly trained, heavily armed bodyguards?

No contest.

Tim knew he didn't have a chance.

The Stanislavian Secret Service would hunt him down and catch him in seconds. And when they caught him, they would hurl him to the ground, cuff his hands together and take him into custody.

That was what should have happened, anyway. And that was what would have happened if Tim and Grk hadn't been so fast, so determined and, most importantly, so small.

Being small has many disadvantages.

You get trodden on. You get ignored. You get forgotten. No one listens when you talk.

But being small has a few advantages too.

You can duck under outstretched arms. You can dodge through crowds. You can scramble under fences. And no one stops you. No one screams. Or yells. Or calls for the police. No one shouts, 'Oi! That hurt! What do you think you're doing?' And no one puts their hands on your jacket and says, 'You pushed my wife! I'd like you to say sorry to her! And I want you to do it right now!'

Tim didn't stop to see who was shouting. Nor did he turn around to see what had happened behind him. He just kept running. He was determined to run and run and run and run and run and run and run and run until a hand grabbed his shoulder or a bullet punctured his lungs.

He didn't worry about Grk. He knew he didn't have to. Grk was perfectly capable of looking after himself. Dodging round legs, springing over bags and galloping through the middle of crowds, Grk never strayed further than a few metres behind Tim and was usually several paces ahead.

They emerged from the crowds and sped towards the road.

Up ahead, Tim could see a bridge and a busy road and a large building. He didn't know where he was going or what he would do when he got there, but he didn't have time to worry about that now. He just ran.

They reached the road. Cars whizzed past. The lights were green, but Tim didn't have time to wait for them to turn red. He charged straight across the road with Grk by his side.

Horns hooted. Brakes screeched. Cars swerved. Tim hoped no one would hit him.

And he was lucky. No one did.

When they got to the other side of the road, Tim could see a choice of four routes. He could run along the road to the left. Or the right. He could go straight ahead and run across the bridge to the other side of the river. Or he could go down the steps.

If he went left, right or straight across, he would have nowhere to hide. His pursuers would catch him easily. That left the steps. He didn't know where they led, but that didn't matter. At least he might have a chance of finding somewhere to hide.

Tim glanced over his shoulder.

He could see a short, stocky, red-faced man coming straight towards him. They were only a few metres apart.

Behind the red-faced man, more bodyguards were sprinting across the road and pouring towards him from every direction.

Tim had a few seconds, nothing more. And then they would get him.

He turned and ran down the stairs. Grk sprinted after him.

At the bottom of the stairs, they both came to a sudden halt, not knowing where to go next. They only had a second to decide. What should they do?

Grk looked at Tim, waiting to see what he did.

Tim looked left. He saw the river and the underside of the bridge. If he went that way, his pursuers would catch him in seconds.

He looked right. He saw a long stretch of pavement without any hiding places. They would catch him immediately that way too.

He looked straight ahead and saw a large boat moored on the quay. It was a cruiser which took tourists along the river to see the sights. The rows of orange seats were packed with people. The boat was just about to leave on its next voyage. Smoke was gushing from the engine. Water was churning. Men were coiling ropes and shouting instructions to one another.

A gangplank stretched between the boat and the shore. As the boat eased away from the shore, two men hauled the gangplank aboard.

That was his only hope.

Tim ran towards the gangplank.

Grk looked at the river, then at Tim. He didn't like water. And he hated getting wet. But he trusted Tim. So he ran after him.

They put their heads down and sprinted at full speed.

The boat moved further from the shore.

Tim reached the bank and hurled himself into the air. Grk did the same. They soared across the water.

For a moment, they seemed to hang in midair, directly above the river. Tim thought he was going to slap straight into the side of the boat. He imagined knocking himself unconscious and slithering into the murky depths. And then he slammed onto the deck, hitting his shoulder and his elbow and his chest, knocking all the breath out of his body.

Grk crashed onto the deck beside him, rolled over in a tangle of legs and came to a halt against the wall.

They lay there, stunned and unable to move, as the boat eased slowly away from the shore and steamed down the Seine.

Tim opened his eyes.

His elbow ached. So did his shoulder. He thought he could feel blood trickling down his forehead.

People were shouting at him. He couldn't understand what they saying, but he didn't care.

It didn't matter. Nothing mattered. Because he was safe.

Grk rolled over and licked his paws.

Tim sat up and looked at the shore.

Colonel Zinfandel's bodyguards were standing there, arguing with one another, each blaming the other for what had just happened. Several metres of water separated them from Tim. He had escaped!

Or so he thought.

But his delight only lasted for a few seconds. Then he realised how stupid he had been.

The bodyguards ran along the shore, keeping level with the boat. They could see Tim. They knew where he was. And, even more importantly, they knew he wasn't going anywhere. As soon as the boat docked, they would be able to come aboard and get him.

He was trapped.

Chapter 26

Colonel Zinfandel jogged along the shore. Four of his men followed him. Others ran along the other bank and took up positions on the bridges, communicating with one another via walkie-talkies.

Colonel Zinfandel loved running. In usual circumstances, he couldn't have imagined anything better than jogging through the centre of Paris, enjoying the fresh air and looking at the most beautiful city in the world.

But these were not normal circumstances.

He had been humiliated by the Raffifis and their friend and their stupid little dog. They had made him look like a fool. So he was determined to catch them. And when he caught them, he was going to kill them – just as he had killed their father and their mother.

Colonel Zinfandel had divided his men into two groups. The first group was searching the Eiffel Tower, checking the lifts and the staircases, looking for the other two children, the boy and the girl, the children of Gabriel Raffifi. The second group, led by himself, was going to hunt down the third boy and the dog.

He remembered meeting the boy in Stanislavia.

The boy had come to the presidential palace and shaken his hand and drunk his orange juice and smiled as if he was perfectly innocent and harmless. Colonel Zinfandel had allowed himself to be fooled. And the boy had repaid him by making him look like an idiot.

Never again, thought Colonel Zinfandel.

This time, he wouldn't be so stupid. This time, he would kill the boy and the dog as soon as he got a chance.

It should have been easy. His men were some of the best soldiers in his army. They had guns and knives. They were fit, energetic and highly trained. They could run a mile in five minutes and kill a man with their bare hands.

How could a boy escape from them?

How could they fail to capture a child and a little white dog?

But there was the evidence for everyone to see. The boy and the dog had somehow managed to leap from the shore to the boat and they couldn't be caught.

Not yet, anyway.

But now his men had surrounded the boat. And the boy and the dog weren't going anywhere.

Colonel Zinfandel's men were positioned all along the Seine. Some were running along the shore. Others were driving down the road. A few were standing on the bridges. Between them, they could keep the boat in sight at all times.

And eventually, when the boat had shown the sights of Paris to a hundred tourists and their cameras, it would have to turn round and return to its dock. The boy would have nowhere to go and no way to escape. He would have to step off the boat and into the arms of the Stanislavian Secret Service.

Colonel Zinfandel smiled.

He was looking forward to that moment. He wanted to get his hands on that boy. And when he got his hands on him, he was going to hurt him.

Colonel Zinfandel stopped running, snapped his fingers and said, 'Binoculars'.

One of his men handed him a pair of binoculars.

Colonel Zinfandel peered through them and focused on the boat.

There was the boy. He was turning his head from side to side, searching for somewhere to go. He looked scared. He knew he was trapped.

And there was the dog too. A little white dog with black patches all over its body.

Colonel Zinfandel grinned. This was fun. He loved hunting. His usual prey were deer and ducks. He didn't often get the chance to hunt boys and dogs. He was going to enjoy catching them.

He handed the binoculars back and started jogging again.

Chapter 27

'*Dix euros.*'

Tim stared at the sailor. 'What?'

'*Dix euros. Pour un billet. C'est gratuit pour les chiens.*'

'I'm sorry,' said Tim. 'I don't speak French. Do you speak English?'

The sailor rolled his eyes. 'You must buy one ticket. For the boat. It will cost ten euros. But the dog, he is free.'

'Oh, sure,' said Tim. 'Here, I'll get my money.' He dug into his pocket and pulled out the envelope of money. He handed over ten euros.

'Thank you,' said the sailor, giving him a pink ticket in exchange.

'*Merci.*' Tim pocketed the ticket. 'Where does this boat go?'

'Along the river.'

'Does it go anywhere near Notre Dame?'

'Of course,' said the sailor. 'There is Notre Dame. You can see it now.' He pointed in the direction that the boat was going. 'There! You see?'

Up ahead, the river divided in two and went around a long, thin island, crammed with trees and buildings. Several bridges connected the island to the mainland. In the middle of the island, there was a thin dark tower, rising into the sky like a needle. Tim pointed at the tower and said, 'Is that Notre Dame? That tower?'

'Exactly,' said the sailor. 'That is the cathedral of our city.'

'Does the boat stop there?'

'No, no,' said the sailor. 'We continue in a circle and return to the place where we started.' The sailor smiled. 'Have a good day, *monsieur. Bon voyage.*' He walked down the boat.

Tim thought about what the sailor had said. He was trapped on the boat. And, even worse, he would be delivered back to the place where he had started. The Stanislavian Secret Service would be waiting for him there. They would grab him, handcuff him and put him in prison. And they wouldn't let him out again until he was dead.

Around him, tourists were staring at the view, pointing out sights and taking photos. None of them spared a second glance for Tim. None of them knew how much danger he was in.

Tim looked down at Grk. 'What are we going to do?'

Grk didn't answer. He wasn't interested. He had more important things to think about.

Further down the boat, a family of tourists were eating a picnic. They had boiled eggs, chopped tomatoes, celery sticks, sliced salami and chicken sandwiches.

Grk stared at the sandwiches, hoping a piece of chicken might fall out and land on the floor. When that happened, he would be ready. He would hurl himself forward, grab the chicken in his jaws and gulp it down before anyone managed to take it back again.

Tim shook his head. He couldn't understand how anyone – even Grk – could be interested in food at a time like this. Didn't he understand that they were in danger? Didn't he know that they were soon going to fall into the hands of Colonel Zinfandel and the Stanislavian Secret Service?

Unless they escaped.

But where could they go? What could they do?

Hiding on the boat would be useless. Colonel Zinfandel's men would search it from end to end and find him easily.

He stared at the river and the shore. His eyes roamed over trees, buildings, boats and bridges.

And then he had an idea.

Chapter 28

Tim waited until the boat went under the arch of a bridge. For a brief moment, they couldn't be seen from the shore.

That would be his chance.

He stared at the mossy bricks above him and the murky water surrounding the boat, then looked around at the other tourists.

None of them gave him more than a glance. They didn't care about a boy and a dog. They were only interested in their picnics and their cameras and one another.

Tim ducked down and grabbed Grk in his arms, then took one last look at the nearest tourists. None of them looked back at him. He could have danced or stripped naked and they wouldn't have noticed.

He didn't want to dance. Or strip naked. He just wanted to get off the boat. Holding Grk with both hands, Tim clambered over the side and slid into the water. Tim took a great gulp of air, then sank under the surface.

The water was icy. It grabbed him and squeezed him and pulled him down. He could feel himself sinking. He struck out with both feet and swam away from the boat. He didn't want to be chopped into pieces by the propellers.

The boat swept past, leaving large waves in its wake, washing back and forth between the river's banks.

Tim and Grk were hurled backwards. They tried to keep their heads above water, but they weren't strong enough. The waves pulled them down. They sank under the surface and disappeared into the bridge's black shadows.

Colonel Zinfandel couldn't believe it.

He stared at the boat with horror and astonishment. The boy had disappeared. But how?

He turned to the soldiers who were standing beside him and yelled, 'What's happened? Where is he? Where did he go?'

No one answered.

No one could see the boy. No one knew where he had gone. And no one dared say so to Colonel Zinfandel. They didn't want to feel the full force of his fury. So they pulled binoculars from their pockets and stared at the boat, searching for any sign of the dog or the boy.

He had been there a moment ago. Everyone had seen him.

He had been standing by the side of the boat, surrounded by tourists. Then the boat went under the bridge. And he disappeared.

When the boat emerged on the other side of the bridge, the tourists were still there, exactly where they had been standing only a few seconds earlier, but there was no sign of the boy.

The dog had gone too.

They had vanished into thin air.

'This is ridiculous,' screamed Colonel Zinfandel. His face was bright red with fury and his fists were clenched. He turned to the men who surrounded him and yelled at them at the top of his voice. 'A boy can't just disappear! Where is he? Where did he go? Someone! Anyone! Tell me! What has happened to that boy?'

Grk hated baths.

Five or six times a year, Natascha ran a bath and put him inside. He always tried to jump out, but he never managed to escape. She kept him in there and shampooed his fur and showered him, then took him out and towelled him dry.

It was horrible.

But this was even worse.

One moment, he had been standing with all four paws on the wooden deck of a big boat, staring at a chicken sandwich, dreaming about dinner. And at the next moment he was in the middle of the biggest bath in the world.

Grk struggled desperately. But however much he struggled, he couldn't escape. Tim was holding him too tightly.

Tim kicked out with all his strength, but he hardly seemed to be moving through the water.

He could feel the current sweeping them under the bridge. They were going to be crushed against the old bricks. His feet pummelled the waves, but they didn't push him hard or fast enough.

Grk was weighing him down. With a small dog in his arms, he couldn't swim properly.

Water went over his head.

Tim was going under.

The river filled his mouth and his nostrils. He coughed and spluttered. He couldn't breathe. He was sinking.

There was only one thing he could do. He twisted round in the water and hurled Grk through the air. He heard a squeal. Then a splash. And then he dipped his head under the waves and swam with all his strength towards the shore.

Without a dog in his arms, he could swim much better. He reached the bank with a few quick, clean strokes. He pulled himself out of the water and collapsed in a sodden heap.

He lay there for a moment, getting his breath back, then stood up. His clothes were sopping wet. A pool of water formed at his feet. But he didn't have time to worry about that now. Colonel Zinfandel would soon realise what had happened. The Stanislavian Secret Service would search both sides of the river. Tim had to get away before they arrived.

And what about Grk? Had he drowned? Or had he been swept down the Seine by the current? Was he now on the other side of Paris? Would they ever see one another again?

All these questions were answered by a sneeze.

Tim turned his head, searching for the source of the sound.

He heard another sneeze. And then another. And then he saw Grk, squatting on the riverbank, shaking his head from side to side.

'Hey!' shouted Tim. 'Hey, Grk! Come here!'

Grk lifted his head, saw Tim, wagged his tail and sneezed again. Then he bounded along the shore, stopped at Tim's feet and sneezed once more.

'Sorry about the swim,' said Tim. 'Have I given you a cold?'

In response, Grk shook himself vigorously from side to side, spraying water in every direction. If Tim hadn't been so wet already, he would have got soaked.

Tim wished he could shake himself like that. A change of clothes would have been nice too. But he was just going to have to get used to being wet. With any luck, his clothes wouldn't take too long to dry in the sun.

'We'd better get going,' said Tim. 'Max and Natascha will be waiting for us.'

Hearing their names, Grk barked excitedly. His tail wagged even faster, spraying dots of water in every direction.

'Yes, I know,' said Tim. 'I want to see them too. Come on. Let's go and find Notre Dame.'

The boy and the dog ran away from the river and headed into the city, leaving a long trail of wet footprints and pawprints on the pavement behind them.

Chapter 29

Tim and Grk plunged through the streets, turning left, then right, then left again, putting as much distance as possible between themselves and the river. Nothing mattered more than escaping from Colonel Zinfandel and his men.

With every step, Tim's wet trousers slapped against his legs and his wet socks slithered backwards and forwards inside his shoes. His wet T-shirt was rubbing against his skin and his wet jumper was starting to stink.

It was horrible.

But he didn't have any choice. Even if he had been carrying a bundle of clean, dry clothes – which he wasn't – he couldn't have spared the time to get changed. If he stopped now, he would get caught. And he was sure that getting caught by Colonel Zinfandel would be a lot more unpleasant than running through the streets in wet clothes.

When they had been running for two or three minutes, Tim turned round and looked back at the way that they had come. He couldn't see anyone. The street was deserted. He stood there for another minute or two, making sure that they were safe, then looked down at Grk.

Grk looked up at him.

Tim said, 'How are you? Still wet?'

Grk wagged his tail. No more drops fell on the

pavement. He had emerged from the river only a few minutes ago, but he hardly seemed to have shaken all the water out of his fur.

'Lucky you,' said Tim. 'I'm soaking.'

He looked around. They were surrounded by tall grey buildings with blue slate roofs. He didn't have any idea where they were or which direction to go.

A woman was walking along the street towards him.

Tim wondered if she was one of Colonel Zinfandel's bodyguards.

She was wearing a blue shirt, white shorts and leather sandals. She had a rucksack on her back and a straw hat on her head. If she was a highly trained, highly armed bodyguard, she was wearing a very good disguise.

Tim tried to remember what Natascha had told him to say.

When the woman came closer, Tim stepped forwards and said, '*Excusez-moi, Madame, où est Notre Dame?*'

'I'm sorry, honey,' said the woman. 'You'd better ask someone else. I don't speak your language.'

'Yes, you do,' said Tim. 'I'm English.'

'Oh, really? That's so funny! I'm an American. Now tell me, honey, when you were speaking French just now, what did you ask me?'

'I'm lost,' said Tim. 'I'm trying to find Notre Dame. But I'll ask someone who actually lives here.'

'Oh, I can tell you how to get to Notre Dame. I've just come from there myself. You have to go down this little alleyway.' The woman pointed to a street on the left. 'Take the first turning on the right. And

115

you'll see Notre Dame right there in front of you. Okay?'

'Thank you,' said Tim. 'That's really helpful'

'It's my pleasure,' said the American woman. She looked at the boy and the dog for a moment, and then said, 'If you don't mind me asking, how did you get so wet?'

'He fell in the river,' said Tim, pointing at Grk. 'And I jumped in to save him.'

'Oh, that's so sweet. You must really love your dog.'

'I suppose I do,' said Tim.

The woman leaned down and patted Grk on his head, then smiled at Tim. 'Goodbye, honey,' she said. 'Have a good day.'

'Thanks,' said Tim. 'And you.'

He and Grk hurried along the street, taking the directions that they had been given by the American woman. They soon found themselves in a large square, bordered by tall buildings on two sides, trees on the third and a large church on the fourth. Tim recognised the spire of Notre Dame.

Hundreds of people were milling around the square, taking photos, buying souvenirs, eating picnics, feeding pigeons, reading guidebooks and staring at the church. Tim scanned the crowd for broad-shouldered men in black suits with gun-shaped bulges under their jackets. He could see some policemen, some traffic wardens, lots of tourists and a few ordinary-looking businessmen in dark suits and sensible ties, but no one who looked like a bodyguard or a soldier. If he was lucky, they would still be following the boat. Perhaps they hadn't yet realised that he had jumped overboard. He whistled to Grk and said, 'Come on, this way. Let's find Max and Natascha.'

Grk wagged his tail.

Together, Tim and Grk jogged across the square and headed towards Notre Dame.

Chapter 30

Tourists and worshippers were queuing to go inside Notre Dame. None of them took much notice of a boy and a girl who were lingering beside the entrance, watching the crowd.

The boy and the girl didn't take much notice of the tourists either. They were scanning the crowd, looking for a boy and a dog.

Max had been the first to arrive. He hadn't been waiting for more than a couple of minutes when he saw Natascha. They embraced and congratulated one another on their good fortune. Both of them had eluded Colonel Zinfandel, escaped from the Eiffel Tower and found their way to Notre Dame.

But where was Tim? And what had happened to Grk?

They stood side by side at the cathedral's entrance, watching the faces of everyone in the crowd, hoping they would soon see Tim – and hoping they wouldn't see Colonel Zinfandel or his men.

Max nudged Natascha and pointed across the square. 'Look! Over there! Do you see?'

Natascha looked up. As soon as she saw what he was pointing at, she jumped to her feet and started running.

Max sprinted after her.

The four of them met in the middle of the square,

surrounded by tourists and pigeons. Tim grinned. Grk wagged his tail and sneezed.

Natascha said, 'You're wet!'

For a moment, Tim thought she had been talking to him, but all her attention was focused on Grk. She knelt on the ground, stroked his fur and said, 'What happened? How did you get so wet?'

'I'm wet too,' said Tim. 'Feel my clothes – they're soaking!'

Natascha seemed to notice him for the first time. 'What have you done to Grk?'

'I haven't done anything to him,' said Tim. 'He fell in the river.'

'Fell in the river? Why? How? What happened?'

'I'll tell you the whole story,' said Tim. 'But first let's get out of here. Colonel Zinfandel can't be far away.'

'Where is he?' said Max.

'When did you see him?' said Natascha.

Tim quickly explained how he had escaped from the Eiffel Tower and where he had last seen Colonel Zinfandel.

'We're on an island,' said Max. 'If they've got any sense, they'll have put a guard on every bridge. They'll have the whole place surrounded.'

'How we can get past them?' said Natascha.

'We don't have to,' said Tim. 'We can go under them.' He reached into his pocket and pulled out the remaining eight métro tickets. They were damp but still usable. 'Let's catch the train.'

*

As they walked across the square, Natascha reached into her rucksack and pulled out the remnants of the bananas and the chocolate. She divided them equally into three portions and handed them out.

'Sorry,' she said, looking down at Grk. 'There's nothing for you. But we'll find you some food later, I promise.'

Grk stared at her with mournful eyes.

'You don't like bananas,' said Natascha. 'And chocolate is bad for you. So don't bother looking at me like that.'

Her words had no effect. Grk watched them with a gloomy expression as they finished off every scrap of banana and every chunk of chocolate too. Then he turned his attention to the pavement, hoping to see a discarded croissant or an old sandwich, dropped by a tourist who had stopped for lunch.

In the corner of the square, they found a map of Paris, showing the locations of the métro stations. A red circle pinpointed their position.

'We're here,' said Tim, pointing at the red circle. 'And the métro is there.' He pointed at a capital M.

The nearest métro station was called Cité. They could reach it without crossing any bridges or leaving the island.

They hurried through the streets, watching the crowds carefully. People sat outside cafés, drinking coffee and eating croissants. Tourists mingled with smart business-men in slick suits. Buskers stood on street corners playing guitars.

And there was the métro.

Ornate green railings surrounded the entrance. Above the stairs, one sign read METROPOLITAN and another announced the name of the station: CITE.

'Let's go,' said Tim. 'It's only seven stops from here to the Gare du Nord. And from there, we're only two hours from London. We'll get home before Mum and Dad realise we've gone.'

They jogged down the stairs to the ticket barriers, where they came face to face with three of Colonel Zindandel's bodyguards.

The three men were wearing black suits and white shirts. They were standing by the ticket barriers, watching everyone who came and went, searching for any sign of the people who had tried to assassinate their leader. They recognised the children immediately.

'Run!' shouted Max.

He turned and sprinted up the stairs.

Natascha, Tim and Grk charged after him.

The three bodyguards were just a few paces behind.

They ran up the stairs and emerged in the streets. There wasn't time to discuss what to do or where to go. Max ran to the left. Tim and Grk ran to the right. But Natascha didn't run anywhere. Before she could move, a bodyguard grabbed her arm and twisted hard.

Natascha screamed. She couldn't help herself. It hurt so much.

Alerted by the noise, Max stopped and turned back.

So did Tim and Grk.

They saw the three bodyguards surrounding Natascha.

'Run!' she shouted to them. 'Leave me here! Save yourselves! Run!'

Max paused for a moment, deciding what to do. Then he walked slowly back to his sister.

Tim and Grk did the same.

They could have saved themselves. But they would have had to leave Natascha behind. And none of them wanted to do that.

One of the bodyguards patted down the three children, searching for weapons. The second opened his jacket, showing the pistol in the holster under his arm, warning the children what would happen if they tried to escape. The third made a call on his mobile, telling Colonel Zinfandel that the assassins had been captured.

Chapter 31

The three bodyguards marched Max, Tim, Natascha and Grk up the stairs, out of the métro and through the streets.

They had been walking for four or five minutes when they came to a row of stairs leading down to the river.

'Go on,' said one of the bodyguards. 'Down there.'

Max went first and the others followed.

They walked down the stairs and found themselves on a narrow concrete dock running alongside the river. They could see a couple of boats, a group of tourists and Colonel Zinfandel.

He was waiting for them on the dock with thirty of his soldiers.

As soon as Max saw Colonel Zinfandel, he darted forwards with his fists raised, hoping to strike a blow against the man that he hated more than anyone else in the entire world.

Before he had taken more than a couple of paces, two bodyguards jumped forwards and intercepted him. One grabbed his right arm and the other grabbed his left. Max struggled desperately, trying to escape, but the bodyguards were stronger than him. They held him back, stopping him from getting anywhere near their leader.

Until Colonel Zinfandel barked an order.

'Let him go,' he said.

Both bodyguards thought they must have misheard. But Colonel Zinfandel said the words again. 'Let him go.'

The bodyguards did as they were told. They released Max. He staggered forwards and stood opposite Colonel Zinfandel.

Every soldier was carrying a gun. Every one of them could have drawn their pistol and shot Max dead. But none of them moved. They waited to see what their leader was planning to do.

Max didn't wait for anyone. He stared defiantly at Colonel Zinfandel and said, 'Are you scared of me?'

'Scared?' Colonel Zinfandel laughed. 'Why would I be scared of you?'

'I don't know,' said Max. 'But if you're not scared, why do you need so many guards? Why can't you face me like a man?'

'I can,' said Colonel Zinfandel. 'And I will.'

'Good. Then send your guards away. Let's fight like men. One against one. You against me.'

Colonel Zinfandel smiled. His white teeth gleamed. 'I admire your courage,' he said. 'And, for that reason, I will fight you. It will be a fair fight. With fists and nothing else. If you win, you can go. You will be free to walk away. You and your sister and your friend and your dog. But if you lose, you will be my prisoners. Does that sound like a good bargain?'

'Yes,' said Max.

'Then let's fight,' said Colonel Zinfandel.

124

Chapter 32

The bodyguards stood in a circle.

Tim, Natascha and Grk joined the circle too.

Max and Colonel Zinfandel paced around the centre of the circle. Their fists were raised. Their eyes never moved from one another's faces. They were ready to fight.

Max was tense, but he didn't show any sign of fear. All his attention was focused on Colonel Zinfandel. He had been waiting for this moment for a long time. He had made a promise to the memory of his parents. He had dreamed about revenge. And this was perfect: fighting Colonel Zinfandel hand to hand was much better than sneaking up on him with a knife. He could hardly wait to start fighting.

Opposite him, Colonel Zinfandel smiled. He felt calm and confident. He knew he was a good fighter and he was sure he wouldn't have any trouble beating Max.

The others watched in silence.

Colonel Zinfandel's bodyguards could have drawn their guns and ended the fight in a moment. But they didn't move. They understood that their leader wanted to settle this particular battle without any help.

Tim and Natascha would have liked to run into the circle to help Max, but they knew he didn't want their assistance. This was his fight. He was determined to win it alone. And if he lost, then he would lose it alone too.

Grk stood at their feet with his ears flat against his skull. The bristles stood up on the back of his neck. He recognised Colonel Zinfandel. He knew his smell. He remembered where they had met before. His lips curled back, showing the shape of his strong, white teeth, and a loud growl came from the depths of his throat.

'Sshh,' whispered Natascha. She leaned down, grabbed Grk and swept him off the ground. She knew what would happen if he attacked anyone now. He would be kicked or punched or even worse. Much better to save his strength and attack Colonel Zinfandel when they actually had a chance of winning. She wrapped Grk in her arms and whispered softly in his ear, telling him to keep calm and be quiet.

Max and Colonel Zinfandel paced around the circle with their fists raised. They watched one another. Round and round they went, each of them waiting for the other to make the first move.

Colonel Zinfandel swung his fist.

Max jumped backwards.

Colonel Zinfandel punched again.

And again Max was quicker. He dodged out of the way. This time, he lunged forward with his arm swinging and tried to take a punch himself.

Colonel Zinfandel didn't duck or jump. He knocked Max's fist aside with one arm, then punched him with the other.

Colonel Zinfandel's fist connected with Max's nose. Max staggered backwards. A thin line of blood ran down his face.

Grk snarled. Natascha gasped and put her hands over her face, covering her eyes. The bodyguards grinned, enjoying the fight.

Max and Colonel Zinfandel circled again, watching one another, waiting to see who would risk the next blow.

Colonel Zinfandel swung his right arm and punched again.

This time, Max tried to dodge out of the way, but he wasn't quick enough. Colonel Zinfandel's fist smacked into the middle of his face.

Max stumbled backwards. Blood was trickling down his forehead. He was breathing heavily and trying to get his balance.

There was an expression of shock on his face. He had been hurt, but he didn't care about the pain. He cared about losing. He wanted to avenge the murders of his parents with his own bare hands, but he didn't seem to be able to do it. His opponent was stronger than him. Colonel Zinfandel had landed two heavy punches and Max hadn't managed a single blow in response.

There was a simple reason for this.

Max was a lean, strong, young man. He played tennis almost every day. But he knew hardly anything about fighting.

His opponent was very different.

Colonel Zinfandel didn't play tennis. He couldn't run very fast. But he loved fighting. He loved kicking, smacking and punching other people. Nothing gave him more pleasure than causing pain to someone else.

127

Every morning, Colonel Zinfandel boxed against the youngest and fittest soldiers in the Stanislavian army. He won almost every fight, leaving his opponents sprawled on the floor with a bloody nose.

Colonel Zinfandel stepped forward. He knew he was winning this fight. He could see the pain in Max's face. Now he wanted to land the final blow. He fought fast and furiously. His fists flew through the air. Left. Then right. Then left again. Wham! Bam! Crash! He pounded Max's face and body, using all his strength to batter his opponent into submission.

There was no way that Max could resist. He simply wasn't strong or skilful enough to fight back. He put up his hands, trying to protect himself, but the blows came too fast. He couldn't resist. He took a step backwards, then another and another, fading under the barrage of blows.

Natascha put her hands over her face, unable to watch, just hoping it would be over quickly.

Tim felt sick. He didn't want to watch, but he couldn't tear his eyes away. He had to see what happened.

Grk quivered, his whole body shaking with emotion.

Finally Colonel Zinfandel swung his right arm and landed a brutal punch in the middle of Max's face.

Max staggered backwards. Blood gushed out of his nose and down his chin. He wobbled on his feet for a moment. He wanted to stay standing and keep fighting. But he didn't have enough strength left in his limbs. He toppled backwards and slumped to the ground and didn't get up again.

Natascha cried out and ran to her brother.

Chapter 33

Max clutched his bleeding nose.

Natascha dabbed his face with her sleeve. She took some plasters from her rucksack and placed them over his wounds. As she worked, she whispered to her brother, asking if he was okay.

Max didn't answer. He couldn't even bring himself to lift his head and look her in the eye.

He had been hit hard. His face hurt. So did his body. But nothing hurt more than the pain of losing.

He would have liked to get up and keep fighting, but he knew there wasn't any point. He was beaten.

He had been dreaming of this moment for a long time. He had been hoping to get the chance to fight Colonel Zinfandel. Just the two of them. Face to face. Man to man. He wanted the chance to take his revenge.

Max was stunned and shocked. He could hardly believe what had happened. He hung his head in shame.

He had been given his chance. And he had failed.

Colonel Zinfandel crossed his arms over his chest and chuckled. There was only one thing that he enjoyed more than fighting – and that was winning. He stepped forward, looked down at Max and Natascha, and spoke to them in Stanislavian.

Tim couldn't understand what Colonel Zinfandel

was saying, but it was clear that his words weren't pleasant. Neither Max nor Natascha replied. They didn't even look at Colonel Zinfandel. But he didn't appear to care. He spoke to them again, then turned his attention to Tim.

'I recognise you,' said Colonel Zinfandel, speaking English with a strong accent. 'We have met before. Your name is Timothy Malt. Am I right?'

Tim nodded. If he had known what to say, he would have spoken back, but he couldn't think of the right words to use.

'We met in my country,' said Colonel Zinfandel. 'You helped these two children – these two criminals – when they escaped from prison. Am I right?'

Tim nodded again.

'I know all about you,' said Colonel Zinfandel. 'I know what you have done. I know you think you are stronger than me. And cleverer than me. But you are quite wrong, Timothy Malt. You may have helped these children before. But you will not be able to help them again. And I have some bad news for you, Timothy Malt. You will not be able to help yourself either.'

Colonel Zinfandel turned and barked an order to his men. They stepped forwards and surrounded the children.

The bodyguards led the children across the grass to the road.

Tim glanced around, searching for a way to escape, but he could see it was hopeless. He was completely surrounded. He wouldn't get further than five paces before one of the guards caught him – or, even worse, shot him.

He would go along with them for now, he decided. He would watch what happened. He would take his time. And later, when the guards weren't guarding him so carefully, he would escape from them. And he would take Max, Natascha and Grk with him.

Three black Toyota Land Cruisers were parked in a row.

The children were ushered into one of the cars and driven away. The other two cars followed close behind, escorting them through the streets of Paris.

Colonel Zinfandel stepped into his own limousine and settled on the long leather seat.

He had more meetings this afternoon. He didn't give another thought to Max, Natascha, Tim or Grk. He knew what would happen to them. He knew they wouldn't escape from him. Later, when his meetings were finished, he would deal with them.

He barked an order to his driver. The limousine eased forward and moved through the traffic.

Tim stared out of the blacked-out window. He could see out, but he knew that no one would be able to see in. There was no point trying to wave or grimace or do anything else to attract the attention of a passer-by.

He glanced at Max and Natascha. Neither of them had said a word since they got into the car. Now they were both staring directly forwards. He wondered what they were thinking about.

131

He looked at Grk, who was crouching on the floor at their feet. He wondered whether Grk was thinking about anything. If so, he was probably thinking about food. That was Grk's main interest in life. Being in a strange car wouldn't make him any different.

Tim remembered that he hadn't eaten for several hours. He was surprised to notice that he didn't feel hungry. Perhaps fear drives out hunger. Because he certainly felt scared.

Until this moment, he realised, he hadn't taken their situation entirely seriously. From the moment that he had been woken up, the whole thing had felt a little like a dream. Coming to Paris had been exciting and dramatic. But this was different. This felt so ordinary that it could only be real.

He wondered where they were going and what might happen when they got there.

He knew what Colonel Zinfandel was capable of. He had already murdered Max and Natascha's parents, so he wouldn't worry about murdering Max and Natascha too. And if he murdered them, he would have to murder Tim and Grk too. Colonel Zinfandel wouldn't want to leave any witnesses who could tell the world what he had done.

I don't want to be dead, thought Tim.

So I'd better think of a way to escape.

Chapter 34

They drove for about twenty minutes through Paris, then turned off the street and plunged down a ramp. The other two cars followed close behind. The ramp led down to an underground car park. Through the darkened window, Tim could see several parked cars and two men wearing leather jackets, standing over a motorbike which they were cleaning or repairing. The men glanced at the car, then went back to whatever they were doing, not interested in anyone or anything else.

They drove down two more levels. There were fewer cars and no people. The whole place appeared to be deserted.

The car stopped. The driver turned off the engine. They sat for a moment in silence. Then the driver turned to the children and barked an order in Stanislavian. Tim couldn't understand what was said, but he followed Max and Natascha when they clambered out of the car. He thought it would probably be best to do whatever they did.

As soon as they climbed out of the car, they were immediately surrounded by Colonel Zinfandel's bodyguards.

Tim looked around and counted the number of men. There were eight. All of them were dressed in black suits and white shirts.

Eight of them, thought Tim. Eight grown men. Fit and strong and probably armed with pistols. Against three of us. Plus Grk.

It's impossible, he thought. We could never escape.

The bodyguards looked calm and happy. It was an easy job for them. They usually spent their lives worrying about assassination attempts, looking out for bullets and bombs, wondering whether they were going to be shot or blown up. Today, they just had to guard three children and a little dog. They were sure that they had nothing to worry about.

There was no sign of Colonel Zinfandel himself. He had come to Paris to meet French businessmen, arms dealers and politicians, and he wasn't going to let his plans be interrupted by the odd assassination attempt.

One of the bodyguards barked another order. Looking at him, Tim decided he must be the leader. He had cruel lips and a small, thin moustache.

He ordered two guards to search the children.

When the guards were sure that the children weren't carrying any concealed weapons, they marched them across the car park, down a dark corridor and into a small lift. The leader pressed the button marked twenty-three. The door slid shut and the lift shuddered upwards.

When they arrived on the twenty-third floor, they walked down a long corridor, passing several flats but no people. They stopped outside at a closed door. Tim noted the number: 238.

The leader knocked twice, paused for a moment and knocked twice more. A voice came from the other side, asking a question. The leader responded and the door opened. Again, Tim couldn't understand what anyone was saying. He wished he understood Stanislavian and hoped he would soon have a chance to speak to Max and Natascha, so they could tell him what had been happening.

They found themselves in the main room of a small apartment. The furniture was anonymous and impersonal. It looked like the type of stuff that you would expect to find in a hotel, not a home.

The three children and Grk were led to a bedroom at the back of the flat. They were ushered inside. One of the bodyguards spoke to Max in Stanislavian, then shut the door. They heard the sound of a key turning in the lock. And they were alone at last.

Chapter 35

As soon as the door was shut, Tim turned to the others and said, 'So what's going on? What did they say?'

Natascha put her finger to her lips. 'Shh.'

'Why?'

Natascha pointed at the walls and whispered, 'They're probably listening.'

Tim nodded. He knew she was right. From that moment onwards, they only spoke in whispers. Tim repeated his questions, speaking so quietly that no one could possibly have overheard what he was saying: 'What's going on? What have they been saying to you? What's happening? Where are we?'

'In a prison,' said Max, choosing only to answer the last of Tim's questions.

'This doesn't look like a prison,' said Tim. 'It looks like an ordinary room in an ordinary flat.'

'It doesn't matter what it looks like,' said Max. 'It's still a prison. We're locked in. We're being guarded by the secret service. They might keep us here. They might even kill us here. But if they don't, they're going to smuggle us out of the country and take us to Stanislavia. And when they get us there, they're going to put us somewhere which really does look like a prison. With bars on the windows and locks on the doors. And we'll never get out of that.'

'We did before,' said Natascha. 'With Tim's help.'

'That was a miracle,' said Max. 'And miracles don't happen more than once in a lifetime. This time, no one will get anywhere near us. The guards won't even let us out of our cells.'

Tim said, 'So what are we going to do? How can we get out of here?'

'We can't get out of here,' said Max. 'We're trapped. We can't escape. It's completely hopeless.' He sighed again. His shoulders slumped. He sat down on the bed and touched his face with his fingers, exploring the extent of his wounds. His cheeks were covered with dry blood and everything hurt.

Natascha sat beside her brother. She licked her sleeve and wiped his face, cleaning the blood from his skin.

While Natascha was tending to Max, Tim looked around the room, taking stock of their situation.

They were locked in a small room on the twenty-third floor of a tower block. They couldn't get out of the door. And even if they did, their progress would be blocked by a group of highly trained and heavily armed bodyguards who would not hesitate to shoot them.

Tim said, 'What about the window?'

Max lifted his head and peered at the window. In a quiet voice, he said, 'What about it?'

'Maybe we can get out of the window and escape from here.'

'Maybe,' said Max. 'But isn't it locked?'

Tim went to the window and saw that Max was right. The window was locked with strong metal bolts. Tim wrenched the bolts, trying to open them, but they were too strong for him.

'We could smash the glass,' said Tim.

'And then what?' said Max. 'Jump?'

Tim pressed his nose to the glass and looked down. He could see a long drop to the ground.

'Twenty-three floors,' said Tim. 'That's a long way down.'

'We can't get out of the window,' said Max. 'And we can't get through the door. I don't imagine we can get through the walls, the floor or the ceiling either. We're trapped.'

'Let's search the room,' said Tim.

Max sighed. 'What's the point?'

'Maybe we'll find something we can use.'

'Fine,' said Max.

It was a small room, but they searched it carefully and methodically, moving from one side to the other, making sure they didn't miss anything. Max looked under the bed. Natascha hunted through the cupboards. Tim ran his fingers along the carpet.

Grk searched the room too. He didn't want to be left out. He scrambled under the bed, ran round the walls and sniffed the floor.

Max found a matchstick. Natascha discovered an empty envelope. Tim didn't find anything. And nor did Grk.

'This is hopeless,' said Natascha. 'There's nothing we can do.'

Max turned on her angrily. 'Hopeless? Hopeless? Don't start complaining now. This is entirely your own fault.'

'My fault? Why is it my fault?'

'Because you came to Paris. Because you followed me. Because you stopped me killing Colonel Zinfandel in the Eiffel Tower. If you'd left me alone, none of this would have happened.'

'If I'd left you alone, you'd probably be dead,' said Natascha.

'I might be,' said Max. 'But I'd be happy.'

'How can you be happy if you're dead?'

'I would have been happy to die. I'd have done what I wanted.'

'That's just stupid,' said Natascha.

'No, it's not,' said Max. 'It's what I wanted most in the world – and you stopped me doing it. All I care about is killing Colonel Zinfandel. Yes, if I'd done it, I might be dead too. Or in a French prison. But you'd be safe. And so would Tim. Rather than all three of us being here. You shouldn't have stopped me.'

'I couldn't let you get killed!' cried Natascha.

'Why not?'

'Because you're my brother.'

'That doesn't matter,' said Max. 'I'm old enough to know what I want to do with my life. I can make my own decisions for myself. You should have left me alone. But you couldn't do that, could you? You had to stick your nose in my affairs. And you've made everything much, much worse.'

Natascha stared at her brother. She couldn't believe what he was saying to her. Why was he so angry with her? Couldn't he understand why she had done what she did?

She had just tried to help him, nothing more. She had thought she was doing the right thing.

She turned away from him, her lower lip quivering, and threw herself on the bed. She didn't want Max or Tim to see that she was crying.

Max walked to the window and stared out. He looked at the view and the long drop to the ground, twenty-three storeys down. He knew he had been horrible to his sister, but he didn't care. He was furious with her – and he wanted her to know it.

Tim didn't want to get involved in their argument. He lay on the floor, stared at the ceiling and kept quiet. He felt cold, hungry, tired and depressed. He didn't understand why Max was so angry with Natascha. He wished they weren't arguing. It made him feel uncomfortable. He didn't know what to do or say. He just tried to keep quiet and wait for them to stop. He lay on the floor, stared at the ceiling and hoped they would be nicer to one another soon.

Grk sat on the floor in the middle of the room and turned his head from side to side, looking from Tim to Max to Natascha and back to Tim again.

Like all dogs, Grk was very sensitive to the moods of humans. He knew when they were happy and when they were sad. Right now, he could tell that Tim, Max and Natascha were miserable. He didn't know why. Nor did he know how to help them. So he simply stared at them with worried eyes, waiting for things to get better.

The room was quiet. No one moved. No one made a sound.

They stayed like that for a long time.

Chapter 36

Mr Malt came home early. He opened the front door, walked into the hallway and called out, 'Hello! I'm home!'

There was no answer.

Mr Malt closed the front door and took off his coat. He wasn't worried about the silence. The children often didn't bother answering when he called out to them.

During the school holidays, Mr and Mrs Malt took turns to come home early. There was no real need for them to do so. They trusted Max. He was old enough to stay at home with Natascha and Tim and make sure nothing went wrong. But the Malts didn't like leaving the three children without an adult for the whole day, so they took turns to come back home from work in the early afternoon.

Mr Malt hung his coat on a hook in the hallway and wondered what the children were doing. The house was quiet, but that wasn't unusual. The house was often quiet in the afternoons. Tim was probably playing a game on his computer. Natascha would be upstairs in her bedroom, reading a book or writing her journal. And Max would be outside in the garden, doing exercises, jogging on the spot or practising his tennis strokes.

But where was Grk?

Even when Tim, Max and Natascha were absorbed in their games and their books, Grk usually charged into the hallway as soon as he heard the sound of the front door. He always wanted to see who had arrived and to check that the house wasn't being burgled.

Today he was nowhere to be seen.

Mr Malt went into the sitting room. He looked around. There was no sign of Grk or the others. He peered into the garden, but they weren't there either. He shouted up the stairs. 'Hello! Tim? Max? Natascha? Are you there? Anyone home!'

There was no answer.

They must have gone for a walk, decided Mr Malt. That was the only explanation. All three children must have gone to the park with Grk.

He went down to the kitchen to make himself a cup of tea. He filled the kettle at the tap and switched it on. While he was waiting for the kettle to boil, he paced across the kitchen, thinking about the work that he had been doing all day.

He had walked back and forth and back and forth and back again when his eyes happened to fall on a piece of paper which had been placed precisely in the middle of the kitchen table. Someone appeared to have written a note. Mr Malt wondered who would have done that – and why. He picked it up and started reading.

Dear Mum and Dad,
I have gone to Paris with Natascha and Grk.
Max is in trouble. We have to help him.

I have taken our passports and Dad's spare
credit card and some euros too.
   Sorry!
   See you later.
   Loads of love from Tim

Mr Malt read the note once more from beginning to
end, then picked up his phone and rang his wife.

She answered immediately. 'Melanie Malt speaking.'

'It's me,' said Mr Malt.

'Hello, Terence. Are you at home?'

'I am,' said Mr Malt. 'And you're not going to believe
what's happened.'

'Oh, no,' said Mrs Malt. 'Not the boiler.'

'No, not the boiler.'

'Not the water tank? Oh, no! Has it leaked again?'

'No,' said Mr Malt. 'It's not the water tank either.'

'Then what is it? Stop being so mysterious, Terence,
and tell me what's happened!'

'It's Tim,' said Mr Malt. 'He's done it again.'

'Oh, no,' sighed Mrs Malt. 'Where's he gone this
time?'

'I don't know. When I came home from work, I found
an empty house and a note from him on the kitchen
table.'

'What about the others?'

'They've gone too. The house is completely empty.'

'What does the note say?'

'If you give me a chance, I'll tell you.'

Mr Malt read the note aloud.

Mrs Malt listened in silence, then let out a long sigh. 'I'd better come home,' she said. 'I'll get there as quickly as I can. Will you ring the police?'

'Of course I will,' said Mr Malt.

He said goodbye to his wife, then put the phone down and read the note once more. He suddenly wondered whether Tim might have been teasing him. It was worth checking. He didn't want to make a fool of himself.

He searched every room from the attic to the basement, checking that his son wasn't hidden in a cupboard or lying under a bed. When he was sure that he was the only person in the house, he had a sudden thought. He went into the sitting room, opened the filing cabinet and took out the file marked TRAVEL.

Inside the file, there was an envelope marked PASSPORTS. Mr Malt opened the envelope. There should have been six passports inside, but there were only two. One for him and one for his wife. The other four had gone.

That was when Mr Malt knew Tim was telling the truth. He really had left the country. There was no point wasting any more time. Mr Malt grabbed his phone again and rang the police.

'I would like to report three missing children,' said Mr Malt.

'Three?' said the policeman on the other end of the line.

'That's right,' said Mr Malt. 'And a dog.'

Chapter 37

The key rattled in the lock. The door opened. One of the guards looked inside and checked what the three children were doing, then went out again and returned a moment later with a wooden tray. He placed it on the floor and walked out again without saying a word. The key rattled in the lock again and then there was silence.

'I suppose that's supper,' said Natascha.

They stared at the contents of the tray. They had been given three glasses of water and a plate of sliced bread. Nothing more.

Grk lifted his head and looked at the others. He was starving. If they didn't want to eat the bread or drink the water, then he would be happy to do so instead. But he wasn't going to take it until they gave him permission.

Tim was the first to move. 'It's better than nothing,' he said, swinging himself out of the chair and crouching on the floor by the tray. 'Come on, let's eat. We'll need our strength later.'

'Why?' said Max.

'Because we might have a chance to escape. And we'll need all our strength if we do.'

'It's not very likely,' said Max. 'We're twenty-three floors up and completely surrounded by armed guards.'

'It's still a chance,' said Tim. 'And a small chance is better than no chance at all. Come on, sit down. Let's eat.'

Tim divided the food into four portions and shared them around. Grk scoffed his bread in one gulp, then lapped water from a glass held by Natascha. The others ate more slowly, savouring every mouthful. They knew that they might not eat again for a long time.

A few minutes later, the guard returned. He took the empty tray away, then told Tim, Max and Natascha that they could take turns to go to the loo. The guard escorted them one by one, taking them through the flat to the loo, leaving the others locked inside the room.

Grk didn't get a chance to pee. He just had to hold it in.

When they had eaten and peed, the guard shut the door again and turned the key in the lock.

Everything was quiet.

Natascha blurted out suddenly, 'What are we going to do?'

'We're going to hope,' said Tim. 'That's all we can do.'

'Hope for what?'

'For a chance,' said Tim. 'For some luck. For something to happen that helps us get out of here. We'll hope for all those things. And maybe we'll be lucky. Now we should sleep.'

'Why?' said Max.

'Because we'll need our strength later. When we try to escape.'

'We're never going to escape,' said Max. 'We're going to be in prison for the rest of our lives.'

'You don't know that,' said Tim. 'We might get a chance to escape. And, if that happens, we have to be strong enough to take it. Come on, let's go to sleep.'

146

Max sighed. He couldn't see any reason to sleep, because he couldn't believe that they would ever get a chance to escape. But he couldn't be bothered to argue with Tim. He lay on the floor and closed his eyes.

Natascha lay on the bed. She knew her brother was right. When they had been in prison before, Tim had rescued them. He had arrived in a helicopter, smashed the prison's walls and liberated every prisoner. He wouldn't be able to do it again. Miracles don't happen twice. This time, Natascha was sure, she and her brother were going to spend the rest of their lives in a small, damp, dark cell. But she didn't bother arguing with Tim. A few moments later, she was fast asleep.

Grk slept too. He didn't know whether things were hopeful or hopeless. He just liked sleeping.

Tim was the only one who didn't sleep immediately. He dipped his hands into his pockets and pulled out everything that he found.

He had eighty-six euros and a few tickets for the métro.

He lay on the floor, staring at the ceiling, and tried to imagine how they could get out of here.

They had a used matchstick, an empty envelope, eighty-six euros and some train tickets.

What could they do with all that?

How could they save themselves from Colonel Zinfandel and all his soldiers?

Chapter 38

Hours passed.

The only sound was the distant noise of a television, booming through the walls from another flat.

Max, Natascha and Tim slept soundly.

Grk slept too, but he lifted his head every few moments, looking around, checking nothing had changed. He was a good guard dog, always ready to protect his owners against trouble. But there wasn't any trouble to be seen, so he dropped his head again and went back to sleep.

In the middle of the night, the key rattled in the lock, the door opened and a guard came into the room. Grk sat up and opened his eyes, staring intently at the guard, but none of the others moved. The noise wasn't loud enough to disturb their sleep. The guard watched them for a moment, saying nothing, then lifted his arms and clapped his hands together.

Now they woke up. Max spun round, his arms raised, ready to fight. Tim rubbed his eyes, groaned and rolled over, wanting to go straight back to sleep. Natascha blinked and looked around with a confused expression as if she couldn't remember where she was.

'Come on,' said the guard. 'Get up. On your feet.' He clapped his hands again. 'Up!'

Tim sat up and said, 'Why do we have to get up? Where are we going?'

'You will find out,' said the guard. 'Come on! Hurry!'

Max and Natascha asked more questions, speaking Stanislavian rather than English, but the guard refused to answer. He wasn't interested in talking to them. He just told the children to gather their possessions and get ready to leave.

They did as they were told. Natascha packed her rucksack. Tim fixed the lead to Grk's collar.

The other guards were waiting for them outside the room. Their faces were stern and expressionless.

The guards took them out of the flat. They went back down in the lift to the underground car park and got into one of the Land Cruisers. Doors slammed. Engines started. No one spoke.

Three big black Toyota Land Cruisers drove out of the underground garage and headed into the streets of Paris.

It was dark and cold, but the streets weren't empty. People were lingering at bus stops or walking quickly, their shoulders hunched, heading to work. No one took any notice of three big black cars, driving in convoy. No one glanced at the darkened windows or wondered who might be sitting inside.

They drove for ten or fifteen minutes, then stopped on a main road. Cars and buses rushed past. The street-lamps cast a yellowish glow. The sky was still dark. The sun wouldn't rise for another two or three hours.

A soldier stepped out, opened one of the back doors and pointed at Tim. 'Get out,' he said. No one moved. He spoke again, louder. 'Come on. I told you to get out. And bring the dog.'

Tim looked at Max and Natascha, then turned back to the soldier and said, 'What about them?'

'They stay. They are not British. They are citizens of Stanislavia. No one cares about them.'

'I'm not leaving them,' said Tim.

'Yes, you are,' said the soldier. 'Come on, get out.' He let his jacket fall open, showing the leather holster that he was wearing.

Tim could see the gun in the holster.

You don't argue with a gun. Not unless you want your head blown off.

Tim turned and looked at Max and Natascha. He didn't know what to do or say. Of course he wanted to get out of the car and escape from the soldiers. But he didn't want to leave his friends behind. He didn't know what was going to happen to them, but he couldn't imagine it was going to be anything good.

'Go,' said Max.

Tim said, 'But what will you do?'

'We'll be fine,' said Max. 'We can look after ourselves.'

Natascha nodded. 'Go on,' she said. 'Go to the police. Or the British Embassy. Tell someone what happened.'

'Okay,' said Tim.

'And look after Grk,' said Natascha. 'Will you do that for me?'

'Of course I will,' said Tim.

'Come on,' snapped the soldier. He was getting impatient. 'No time for talking. Get out! Or I might change my mind and take you too.'

Tim clambered out of the car. He tugged Grk's lead.

150

Grk leaped down from the car and stood on the pavement beside him. They stared into the car at Max and Natascha, who stared forlornly back again.

Grk's tail was down between his legs. He didn't understand what was happening, but he knew he didn't like it.

The soldier slammed the door, locking Max and Natascha inside the car. Tim couldn't see them now. They were hidden behind the darkened windows.

'Goodbye,' said the soldier and marched round the car.

Tim said, 'Where am I?'

'Paris,' said the soldier. He opened the door and got inside.

Tim said, 'What am I meant to do?'

'You can do what you like,' said the soldier. 'You are free.'

'Why have you let me go?'

'You are British citizen,' said the soldier. 'We cannot take you out of France. But these two . . .' He jerked his thumb in the direction of the car, pointing at Max and Natascha. 'They are citizens of Stanislavia. They are our people. With them, we can do whatever we want.'

Before Tim could ask another question, the soldier slammed the door. The engine roared. The car eased forward. The other two cars followed it. They rejoined the traffic and drove away.

Tim and Grk didn't move. They just stared at the three big black cars as they accelerated down the road.

*

151

Inside the car, no one said a word.

Max looked at Natascha.

Natascha looked at Max.

And then both Max and Natascha turned their heads and looked out of the back window. They could see Tim and Grk standing on the pavement.

Getting smaller and smaller as the car drove down the street.

Then the car turned a corner and they were gone.

Max and Natascha glanced at one another once more. Each of them would have liked to say something. But both of them knew that whatever they said would be overheard by the soldiers in the car. And neither of them wanted that to happen. So they faced forward and kept quiet.

The car drove quickly through the streets of Paris.

Chapter 39

Tim was alone.

No, not completely alone.

He looked at Grk and said, 'What are we going to do now?'

Grk looked back at him with a mournful expression. Grk didn't understand what was happening. Why had Max and Natascha gone away? Where were they going? And when was he going to see them again?

Tim didn't know the answer to any of these questions. He lifted his head and looked around, wondering where he was and what he should do next.

It was dark, cold and wet. There were a few people wandering through the streets. Some of them gave Tim a curious glance, wondering what a boy was doing out at this time of the morning, but most of them were occupied by their own thoughts. It was too early to worry about other people.

Tim thought through his options. He could stop a policeman and ask for help. He could try to find the British Embassy. Or he could ring his parents. He wondered what they were doing at the moment. He hadn't thought about them for hours. They must have found his note by now. Would they be worrying about him? Would they have followed him from London to Paris? Perhaps they weren't very far away.

He dug his hands into his pockets and pulled out the envelope of money. He looked inside. He had eight métro tickets and a handful of euros.

Eighty-six euros. That's how much he had. He remembered counting them in the flat.

What was he going to do with eighty-six euros?

He could buy himself breakfast. He could get the métro and go to the British Embassy. Or he could just stop a taxi and tell the driver to take him to the nearest police station.

A taxi, thought Tim.

He suddenly knew exactly what he wanted to do. He wasn't interested in breakfast. He didn't care about finding the police or the British Embassy. He jumped off the pavement, lurched into the middle of the street and stuck out his hand.

He had seen a car driving towards him. It was a silver Mercedes with a small sign on the roof which said TAXI.

The taxi stopped.

Tim opened the door, climbed into the front seat, put Grk at his feet and said, 'Follow that car.'

The driver said, 'Pardon, *monsieur*?'

'Follow that car,' repeated Tim.

'You wish for me to follow a car?' said the driver, speaking English with a strong French accent.

'Yes!' said Tim. 'I've told you twice already!'

'But, *monsieur*, there is one important question. Which car do you want me to follow?'

Tim looked at the road ahead. There were ten or

154

fifteen cars to be seen, but none of them was a big black Toyota Land Cruiser belonging to the Stanislavian Secret Service. 'Go down there and turn right. You'll soon see the car. I'll point it out as soon as I can.'

The driver shrugged his shoulders and started driving. He said, 'You are English?'

'Yes,' said Tim.

'You are a detective, perhaps?'

'No,' said Tim.

'Then why do you want to follow this car?'

'My friends are inside. They've been kidnapped.'

The driver raised his eyebrows. 'Really? This is true?'

'Yes, it is,' said Tim. 'It's all true, I promise.'

'Then we must find them,' said the driver. 'Hold tight.'

The driver rammed his foot on the accelerator. The car sprang forwards and shot down the street. Grk was thrown backwards. Tim held onto his seat with both hands. He was glad to be wearing a seat belt. If they crashed, he didn't want to go through the windscreen.

The driver grinned. He didn't often have an opportunity to drive like this. He usually took drunks home from a bar or delivered old women to the hairdresser. He had always wanted to be involved in something as exciting as a car chase in a movie. And this was his big chance.

With a squeal of tyres, the taxi turned the corner. There were several cars ahead. The driver glanced at Tim, who shook his head.

'No problem,' said the driver. 'We will catch them.'

He accelerated through the traffic, careering down the road at full speed.

Without taking his eyes from the road and leaving his left hand on the steering wheel, the driver offered his right hand to Tim. 'My name is Yusef,' he said.

'My name is Tim,' said Tim, taking Yusef's hand and shaking it very quickly. Yusef was a good driver, but even the best drivers can hardly shake hands and drive at the same time.

'Nice to meet you, Tim,' said Yusef. 'Welcome to Paris.'

To Tim's relief, Yusuf put both hands on the steering wheel and concentrated all his attention on driving.

They drove in and out of the traffic. Horns blared and angry drivers waved their fists, but Yusef didn't care. He was having too much fun.

Little streets went off to the right and left, but Yusef stayed on the main road, heading out of Paris. It was a risk – the Stanislavian Secret Service might have driven on a different route – but it seemed a risk worth taking. They drove for a few minutes, overtaking other cars, and then Tim shouted, 'There! That's them!'

Yusef peered through the windscreen at the line of traffic ahead. 'That one? The Toyota?'

'There are three of them,' said Tim. 'Can you see?'

'Ah, yes,' said Yusef. 'I see them now. Come on, let's catch them.' He urged his taxi forward, weaving through the traffic, coming closer and closer to the convoy of three big black cars.

Chapter 40

Yusef had never followed a car through the streets of Paris before, but he knew exactly what to do. He had seen lots of chases in movies. He stayed close enough that he could always see the three big black cars, but he never went too close, not wanting them to realise that they were being followed.

When they had been driving for a few minutes, Yusef turned to Tim and said, 'You must tell me one thing, *mon ami*. Who is driving in the car? Why is it so important for you to follow them?'

Tim wondered whether he should invent some story, then decided that there was no point. Why not just tell the truth? So he told Yusef everything. He explained how Max and Natascha had been thrown in prison with their parents, and how the Raffifis had been murdered by Colonel Zinfandel, and how he had met Grk in the street, and how he and Grk had got from London to Stanislavia. He described how Max and Natascha had come to live with him and his parents in London. And then he explained what had happened less than twenty-four hours ago, when he had been lying in his own warm, comfortable bed, dreaming about this and that, when Natascha woke him up and told him that Max had disappeared, leaving nothing but a mysterious letter and no clues

157

except a few words scrawled on a screwed-up piece of paper.

When Tim had described the events of the last twenty-four hours, Yusef nodded. 'You don't have to worry,' he said. 'These people – we will catch them. And we will get your friends. And you will all be able to go home safely. Okay?'

'Thank you,' said Tim. '*Merci beaucoup.*'

'Ah,' said Yusef. 'You speak French?'

'No. I can say "*merci beaucoup*" and "*où est Notre Dame*" and "*fromage*" and "*pomme*", but not much else.'

'Then I will teach you,' said Yusef. 'Speak after me and you will learn very good French. And when you are speaking good French, you can teach me to speak good English. Okay?'

'Sure,' said Tim. 'It's a deal.'

That was how Tim and Yusef spent the next hour as they drove through the outskirts of Paris and plunged into the countryside, following the three big black cars. Yusef said French phrases aloud and Tim repeated them again and again until he could say them correctly.

Tim had learnt a little French at school, but he always forgot a word as soon as he heard it. For some reason, learning a new language from a taxi driver was much easier than learning in a class packed with other students. Tim could soon ask for a drink, say his name and explain where he had been born, all in fluent French.

They drove through the countryside. The rain rattled on the windscreen. The road twisted and turned. There were

158

no other cars to be seen. Tim hoped that the Stanislavian Secret Service wouldn't notice that they were being followed by a silver Parisian taxi.

He wondered where they were going. What if they were driving all the way back to Stanislavia? How far would Yusef take him? And if Yusef got tired or bored and decided to drop him and Grk by the side of the road, what would they do next?

He worried about money. He had eighty-six euros in an envelope. How would he pay Yusef for driving him so far? When Yusef discovered that he wasn't going to get paid enough, how would he react? Wouldn't he be angry? Would he turn round and drive back to Paris and deliver Tim to the police?

Tim soon discovered the answers to all his questions. The three cars didn't drive all the way from Paris to Stanislavia. They drove through the countryside, taking small roads, and soon reached their destination.

There was a tall fence on their right. Tim could see lights and big buildings on the other side of the fence.

'I know this place,' said Yusef. 'It is a private airport. I have been here to collect a passenger and bring him back to Paris.'

The convoy stopped at the entrance to the airfield, but Yusef kept going. If they stopped too, they would be spotted immediately and their presence would be questioned.

When they were out of sight, Yusef parked his car by the side of the road and looked at Tim. He said, 'I can take you back to Paris. Or we can wait here and see what happens. What do you want to do?'

Tim thought for a moment. He went through the possible options in his mind. Then he told Yusef exactly what he wanted to do.

Yusef smiled. 'You are a very brave boy.'

'No, I'm not,' said Tim. 'I don't want to be here. I didn't even want to get out of bed yesterday. But now I'm here, I have to help my friends.' He reached into his pocket, pulled out the white envelope and handed it to Yusef. 'That's all my money,' Tim said. 'It's only eighty-six euros. I know it's not enough to pay you for driving me all the way out here. But I've written my address and my phone number on the envelope. If you ring my parents, they'll pay you the rest.'

'Don't worry about the money,' said Yusef. 'Just go and get the bad guys.'

The taxi drove along the road and parked beside the gate that led into the airfield.

It was raining hard and Yusef hunched over as he ran from his car to the hut. He peered through the window. The guard was inside, sitting on a wooden chair, staring at television screens which showed the entire airfield. Yusef called out to him. '*Mon ami! Mon ami!*'

The guard pushed back his chair and came to the window. '*Oui?*'

They talked briefly. Yusef said he was looking for a passenger who had rung him, asking to be picked up from the gate.

The guard checked his schedule and shook his head.

He said that there wouldn't be any passengers at the airport until later in the day.

While they were talking, the guard never bothered turning his head to look at his television screens, so he didn't see that the cameras had captured two intruders entering the airfield. Nor did he notice two shadowy shapes darting through the undergrowth and ducking under the barrier.

When Yusef was sure that Tim and Grk were safely inside the airfield, he thanked the guard, apologised for wasting his time and said he must have been mistaken about his passenger.

Yusef hurried through the rain to his car and jumped inside.

He drove back to Paris with a smile on his face.

Chapter 41

Tim and Grk ran across the tarmac.

Tim kept expecting someone to shout at him, ordering him to stop and put his hands in the air, but he didn't hear anything except the whistling wind and the rattle of the rain.

He could see big buildings on both sides. He was sure they were aircraft hangars. Up ahead, he could see a runway. A plane was waiting to take off. Lights glowed in the windows. That must be where the soldiers had taken Max and Natascha. Tim changed direction and headed for the plane. Grk galloped alongside him.

The rain was coming down harder now. Tim was getting wetter with every step. Water streamed down his face. His clothes were sodden. But he kept going. He had been soaked to the skin once already in Paris and he didn't care about a little more water now.

He could see several cars parked beside the plane. As he came closer, he recognised them. There were the three big black Toyota Land Cruisers which had escorted Max and Natascha out of Paris. And there was a big black limousine.

So Colonel Zinfandel was here too.

Tim felt a sudden jolt of fear. He remembered his warm bed and his comfortable duvet. He wondered what he was doing here, running across the middle of a

162

French airfield, soaked to the skin, throwing himself at the mercy of a cruel tyrant and his private army.

Then he told himself to stop worrying. His friends were in danger. He had to help them. It was as simple as that.

He pushed all these thoughts out of his mind and tugged the lead. Grk wagged his tail. They ran across the tarmac and headed for the plane.

There was no shelter. They couldn't hide. Tim just hoped that the rain and the gloom would hide them from any enquiring eyes.

Where were Max and Natascha? What had happened to the soldiers who were guarding them? And where were the drivers? Had they all gone into the plane? If so, what were they going to do with their cars? These questions ran through his thoughts, but there was no time to worry about them now. He would discover the answers soon enough. For now, he just had to concentrate on running as fast as possible – and not being seen.

They reached the nearest car.

Tim ducked behind the car, pulling Grk after him, then poked his head around the side.

He could see the flight of stairs which led into the plane. Two soldiers were standing at the bottom of the stairs. The tips of their cigarettes glowed in the darkness. They didn't appear to have seen him.

Max and Natascha must be inside the plane. Colonel Zinfandel would be there too. He would be planning to fly them back to Stanislavia. When he got there, he would put them in a deep, dark dungeon and never let them out.

163

Tim knew what he had to do: he had to climb up the stairs and sneak inside the plane. Otherwise he would never see Max and Natascha again. But how could he get past two armed men?

He couldn't fight them. He couldn't distract them. He couldn't sneak past them. So what was he going to do?

And then the decision was made for him.

Grk sneezed.

Grk was a small dog with a small nose, but he made a surprisingly loud noise when he sneezed.

Tim looked down at him and hissed, 'Sshhh!'

But he was too late. The guards had heard the sneeze. They looked at one another, threw their cigarette butts onto the tarmac and hurried forwards.

Tim watched them coming towards him.

They came closer and closer, heading directly towards him.

Just before they reached him, Tim turned and ran round the other side of the car. He ducked down, keeping low, hoping they wouldn't notice him in the darkness.

He heard voices shouting to one another in a language that he couldn't understand.

He could tell where the voices were coming from. They were behind him. They had reached the place that he had been standing just now. He sprinted forwards, darting between the cars, and approached the plane.

He looked up the flight of stairs.

If he went up there, he would find himself in the belly of the plane. He would be throwing himself into the hands of Colonel Zinfandel. He would never escape.

But if he didn't go up those stairs – if he turned and ran into the darkness – he would never see Max and Natascha again.

Never looking back, he scrambled up the stairs and sprinted into the plane. Grk ran alongside him.

Behind them, the soldiers searched every car. They opened the doors. They peered through the windscreens. They kicked the wheels. But they didn't find anyone.

Tim and Grk stood at the top of the stairs and looked around.

Water dripped from Tim's clothes and Grk's fur, forming a pool on the floor.

They were standing at the back of the plane. Tim could see a door to the left, another to the right and a third straight ahead. He could hear voices. He knew he had to move fast if he wasn't going to get caught. But where should he go?

One of the doors opened.

Tim ducked to the left, dodging out of the way before he could be seen. He pulled Grk after him. They scrambled along the floor. Behind him, Tim could hear voices getting louder. He couldn't understand what was said.

He found himself in the kitchen. He could see a row of cupboards. He opened the nearest. It was stacked with plates and glasses.

He closed the door and opened the next one. It was a fridge, packed with bottles of wine and cartons of orange juice.

165

He slammed that door and opened the next one. There were some plastic bags inside. Tim pushed them back and made just enough room to fit a boy and a dog.

Tim threw Grk inside, squeezed into the cupboard after him and pulled the door behind them. It closed with a click.

They squatted in the darkness.

Tim's neck was bent. His arms were twisted. His legs ached. He felt horribly uncomfortable. But at least he was safe.

For now.

He heard voices and footsteps. They got louder. Two people had come into the kitchen. If they opened the cupboard, they would see him immediately.

But they didn't. The voices continued, but the footsteps stopped. Whoever they were, they were now sitting down.

Tim heard two clicks. He recognised the sounds. People were strapping themselves into their seat belts. The plane must be preparing for take-off.

A massive roar filled his ears. The engines had been switched on.

The plane juddered and rolled slowly forwards along the tarmac.

A few seconds later, they were airborne.

Chapter 42

Mr Malt was woken in the middle of the night by the sound of a ringing phone. For a moment, he thought he was dreaming. Then he remembered what had happened yesterday. He sat up and grabbed the phone. 'Yes?' he said. 'Yes? Who is it?'

A voice spoke in a strong French accent. 'Am I speaking to Monsieur Malt?'

'Yes,' said Mr Malt. 'Who are you?'

'My name is Yusef. I have a message for you.'

Mr Malt had hardly slept. He and his wife had spent most of the night talking to the police and one another, trying to imagine where Tim, Natascha and Max might have gone. He was exhausted. But he still snapped to attention when he heard what the Frenchman was saying. He said, 'What's happened? Where's Tim? Have you taken him?'

'Yes, I have taken him,' said Yusef.

'You've kidnapped my son?'

'No, no,' said Yusef. 'I don't kidnap him. I take him in my taxi.'

Mrs Malt sat up, rubbing her eyes. She said in a soft voice, 'Who is it? What's happening? Have they found Tim?'

Mr Malt shook his head, then spoke into the phone. 'Can you explain exactly what you meant by what you just said? Have you seen my son, Tim?'

'I just told you, I take him in my taxi,' said the voice on the other end of the phone. 'Of course I see him. How can I take him in my taxi if I don't see him?'

Mr Malt said, 'You're a taxi driver?'

'Yes, I drive a taxi in Paris. My name is Yusef. Your son – he is a very brave boy.'

'But where is he now?'

Yusef spoke English badly, so the explanation took a long time, but he did eventually manage to explain what had happened. He told Mr Malt how he had found Tim by the side of the road in the centre of Paris and delivered him to a private airfield in the countryside.

Mr Malt wrote down Yusef's name, address and phone number, thanked him again and said, '*au revoir*'.

He put down the phone and explained everything to his wife. Then he rang the police and told the whole story all over again.

The police worked fast.

They alerted the French authorities to the fact that a boy had disappeared. He had last been seen at a private airfield on the outskirts of Paris. A taxi driver had dropped him at the gates.

The French police interrogated the airfield's flight controllers. Had anyone seen the boy? Could he have boarded a plane? How many planes had taken off that morning? And where had they been going?

The flight controllers sent messages to every plane that had left the airfield.

168

'A boy has disappeared,' said the message. 'He may have sneaked aboard your plane. Are you carrying a stowaway? Do you have any unexpected passengers? Please check immediately.'

The answers came back promptly.

No one had seen a boy. None of the planes was carrying any unexpected passengers. They had checked their passengers and their cargos and they didn't have any stowaways.

Tim had disappeared.

Chapter 43

Peanuts. Orange juice. In-flight movies. Comfortable seats. Safety announcements. A sick bag.

Tim had been given all these things on planes.

But today was very different. Today he didn't get offered anything at all. He just sat in a small cupboard and hoped no one would find him.

He was extremely uncomfortable.

His body was contorted into a strange shape. His clothes were wet and he was sitting in a pool of water which had dripped off him.

He wanted a drink. He wanted a pee. He wanted to stretch his legs. More than anything, he wanted to get out of the cupboard and move around. But he didn't dare move.

The engines were so loud that he couldn't hear anything else. He couldn't see anything either. Several soldiers might have been standing an arm's-length away and he would never have known about them.

Grk was much more comfortable. He usually slept in a small basket, so he was used to confined spaces. He didn't even mind being aboard an aeroplane. He simply curled up and went to sleep.

The plane climbed for a few minutes, then flattened out and the engines quietened. They were thirty thousand feet above the ground and would cruise at this altitude until they reached their destination.

Tim knew he had to move. The flight attendants would start serving drinks soon. If he stayed here, someone would open the cupboard, looking for a bottle or some peanuts, and he would be caught. But where should he go? And what should he do?

First he had to get out of the cupboard. Then he could decide where to go and what to do.

He pushed the door. It swung open.

He waited for a couple of seconds to see if anyone shouted or screamed, alerted to the presence of an intruder, but the only noise was the low hum of the engines. So he thrust himself forwards, put his head out of the cupboard and had a quick look around. To his relief, he couldn't see anyone. He clambered out and stood up, stretching his arms and legs, trying to get the blood flowing round his body again.

Grk scrambled after him and darted round the kitchen, sniffing the cupboards and the floor. He could smell food. And he hadn't eaten for a long time. He pressed his nose against the nearest cupboard. To his irritation, he couldn't get the door open.

Tim looked around, taking stock of his surroundings. The narrow kitchen was empty, but he couldn't stay here. Someone would be sure to come along in a moment.

There were two exits, left and right.

Tim chose left.

He found himself in a corridor. To his left, he could see the main body of the plane and the backs of several heads. People were sitting in the seats, facing

171

forwards. If anyone turned around, they would see him immediately.

No expense had been spared on the creation of the presidential plane. Everything had been built from the finest materials. The large leather seats had plump cushions and wide headrests. A huge TV screen was fixed to the wall. Little wooden tables held drinks and snacks. The plane didn't even feel like a plane. You could imagine you were actually standing in a normal room in a normal house, filled with comfortable chairs and elegant furniture, rather than travelling through the air at supersonic speed, thirty thousand miles above the ground.

Tim knew he couldn't go forwards into the main cabin. He would be caught immediately. So he turned round and looked the other way.

He could see two doors. One led to a toilet. Another was unmarked.

He could lock himself in the toilet. He would be safe there for a few minutes. Maybe even an hour. But people would eventually guess that something was wrong. They would realise that someone had locked themselves inside. And when they broke the door down, Tim would have nowhere to run.

So there was only one place that he could go. Through the unmarked door. He didn't know what was on the other side, but he would have to take the risk and find out. He grabbed the handle and took a deep breath. Then he turned the handle, opened the door and went inside.

He found himself in Colonel Zinfandel's private office.

He saw a huge plasma screen fixed to one wall, showing news footage from CNN. He saw a woman sitting at a desk and typing on a laptop. He saw two soldiers lounging on a leather sofa. And he saw Colonel Zinfandel.

All four of them looked up and stared at the boy standing in the doorway.

For a moment, no one moved. They were all too surprised to react.

Tim was the first to recover. He darted backwards, pulling the door after him, slamming it shut.

He heard shouts and movement on the other side of the door.

He looked around, wondering what to do.

He could hide in the toilet. But they would easily find him there.

Or he could sprint into the main cabin and try to find a hiding place there. But it was packed with men and women from the Stanislavian Army and the Secret Service. They would grab him as soon as they saw him and pin him to the ground.

So what should he do? Where should he go?

The door opened. Colonel Zinfandel emerged. He was carrying a pistol in his right hand. He looked left, then right, then left again, but he couldn't see any sign of the boy. He yelled at his guards, alerting them that there was an intruder on the plane.

173

Men jumped to their feet. Some shouted orders. Others sprinted forwards, drawing their weapons. They covered every exit.

Colonel Zinfandel had spent a lot of money on his private jet, buying one of the best models on the market, but it was still a small, confined space. There was an office, a TV room, a bathroom and a kitchen. And that was all. On such a small plane, there was nowhere to hide.

So where was the boy?

Following Colonel Zinfandel's orders, the soldiers spread out and searched the plane from end to end.

Down at the far end of the plane, Max and Natascha looked at one another with wild excitement in their eyes.

Natascha said, 'Do you hear what they said?'

'There's a boy on the plane,' said Max.

'You know who that must be!'

Max nodded. 'Tim's here.'

'How did he get here?' said Natascha.

'That's not important,' whispered Max. 'Only one thing matters. How can we help him?'

Chapter 44

Tim and Grk were crammed inside the cupboard.

It felt familiar. They had hidden here before.

But it felt different too. They could hear shouts and footsteps. The plane was full of activity. People were running around, searching for them. In a minute or two, someone would look inside the cupboard. And then what would happen?

Tim had prepared himself for that moment. His arms were pressed against the side of the cupboard. His legs were tensed.

He was ready.

There were six soldiers on the plane.

Two went forwards to the cockpit and guarded the pilot. They didn't want anyone coming into the cabin and trying to disrupt the flight.

The other four soldiers went through the entire aircraft, checking every room, looking for the intruder. One of them searched under the seats in the cabin. Another went through the overhead lockers. A third checked the toilet. The fourth went into the kitchen.

He opened the fridge, but there was nothing inside except bottles of wine and cartons of orange juice.

He opened the next cupboard and found forty glasses.

He opened another cupboard – and a shoe caught him

between the eyes.

'Arrgghh!' cried the soldier and staggered backwards.

Another shoe smacked him in the chest, knocking the breath from his lungs. And then several small sharp white teeth bit into his ankle.

The shoes belonged to Tim. He had been waiting in the cupboard, his legs tensed, preparing himself to kick the first person who opened the door. The teeth belonged to Grk. As soon as he saw the soldier, he leaped forward and took a big bite out of his ankle.

The soldier writhed on the floor.

Tim and Grk jumped over him and ran into the corridor. They looked both ways, then dodged back again. But they weren't quick enough. They had been seen already.

A shout went up. Then another. Soldiers came running.

Tim darted through a doorway. Grk ran alongside him. They charged into Colonel Zinfandel's private office. And then they stopped.

They were facing the barrel of a gun.

Colonel Zinfandel was standing right in front of them. He was wearing a black suit and pointing a pistol at Tim's forehead.

'Timothy Malt,' he said with a smile. 'What an unexpected pleasure. Would you mind putting your hands in the air?'

Tim did exactly what he was told. He raised his hands into the air. He knew that there was no point disobeying a man with a pistol. Not unless you want a bullet in your head.

Chapter 45

Colonel Zinfandel stared at Tim and smiled.

Tim stared back. He didn't smile. He just tried not to look scared.

Down at his feet, Grk growled. It was a deep, low growl which could hardly be heard above the noise of the engines.

'You are very stupid,' said Colonel Zinfandel. 'You should have taken your chance when I gave it to you. I told my men to let you go. They dropped you in the street. Why didn't you stay there? Why have you followed me?'

'I didn't follow you,' said Tim. 'I followed Max and Natascha.'

'And why have you done that?'

'Because I wanted to help them,' said Tim.

'You haven't helped them,' said Colonel Zinfandel. 'And you haven't helped yourself either. Now all three of you are going to die.'

'You can't kill us.'

'Of course I can,' said Colonel Zinfandel. 'This is my plane. I can do whatever I want. If I want to kill you, I will kill you. In fact, I'm going to do it right now.'

Colonel Zinfandel's finger tightened on the trigger.

Tim stared at the black mouth of the pistol.

A white shape flashed across the room.

Colonel Zinfandel cried out and staggered backwards.

Grk had recognised the smell of Colonel Zinfandel. He knew he hated him. And he wanted to do something about it.

So he clamped his jaws around Colonel Zinfandel's ankle.

Colonel Zinfandel looked down at the dog attached to his ankle. He twisted his arm and pointed the pistol at the ground.

He fired.

A loud bang echoed through the room.

A hole appeared in the floor. Colonel Zinfandel had missed. It was difficult to shoot Grk without hitting his own foot. He aimed again.

But before he could shoot a second time, Tim hurled himself across the room and grabbed his arm.

They struggled desperately over the gun.

Colonel Zinfandel was a strong man. A dog was biting his ankle and a boy was wrestling his arm, but he could cope with both of them. He gritted his teeth, looped his left arm around Tim's neck and pointed the gun. Then he pulled the trigger again.

BANG!

A hole appeared in one of the windows. The bullet had smashed straight through the glass.

WHOOOOSHH!

Air was sucked out of the cabin.

Papers whirled off the desk. Paintings lifted from the walls. Clothes and crockery went flying.

Tim, Grk and Colonel Zinfandel rolled across the floor in a frenzy of feet and fists and teeth. Each of them was fighting for survival. Whoever won would live. Whoever lost would die.

Grk bit down with all the strength in his jaws.

Tim struggled till his muscles felt like stones.

Colonel Zinfandel kicked and punched and twisted round. He couldn't see where the gun was pointed. But he pulled the trigger anyway.

There was a scream and a yell and a bark and a growl and a loud explosion – all at the same time.

'Arrrrgh!' cried a voice.

And the three of them rolled apart.

Tim was lying on the floor. There was a terrible noise. Like rushing wind. As if he was trapped inside a storm.

He could feel all kinds of awful pains in his arms and his legs. And he could feel something else too, something even worse.

Something wet.

He touched the wetness, then lifted his hand to see what he had touched.

His fingers were coated with red liquid. He knew immediately what it was. Of course he did.

He was bleeding. His belly was soaked with blood.

He was dying.

But...

It was very strange...

He didn't feel as if he was dying.

179

His arms hurt. His legs hurt too. His head hurt. Even his feet hurt. All of them were battered and bruised. But he didn't feel as if he was dying.

Maybe I'm in shock, thought Tim. Maybe my body doesn't know it's dying. Maybe this is how people always feel when they're just about to die.

Or maybe ...

He sat up and looked around.

The room was chaotic. Papers and clothes and cups and spoons had flown through the air, pulled towards the shattered window by the change in pressure. Some of them had been sucked outside. Others had been plastered to the window, blocking the hole in the glass.

Grk was lying on the floor, licking his paws.

There was another body on the floor too. A man in a black suit. His white shirt was covered with blood. His open eyes were staring at the ceiling. He wasn't moving or breathing.

Colonel Zinfandel was dead.

Tim touched the blood on his own belly. Now he understood what had happened.

The blood wasn't his. It was Colonel Zinfandel's.

When Colonel Zinfandel fired his gun, he had shot himself.

Chapter 46

The soldiers raised their guns.

They were Colonel Zinfandel's special bodyguards. They had served him faithfully for many years.

And now he was dead.

They looked at the boy who had killed him.

Tim stared back.

He knew he couldn't fight them.

He could have grabbed Colonel Zinfandel's gun, but even a gun wasn't much use against an army of highly trained, highly armed bodyguards. Especially if you didn't really know how to use it.

He put his hands into the air.

Grk stared at the soldiers too. He was ready to carry on fighting. He was even ready to die if he had to. He opened his mouth, showing his sharp, white teeth, promising to take a big bite of anyone who came close.

One of the soldiers stepped forwards. Grk growled softly and the bristles stood up on the back of his neck, but the soldier took no notice. He walked to Tim, raised his right hand and said, 'Thank you.'

'For what?' said Tim.

'You have done a great thing,' said the soldier. 'You have killed the worst leader we ever had.'

Tim looked at the soldier's hand. Then he took it in his own and shook it.

One by one, the other soldiers walked forward and shook Tim's hand. They shook hands with Max and Natascha too. Some of them kneeled on the floor and tickled Grk's ears.

'Thank you,' said the soldiers in English and Stanislavian. 'Thank you for saving our country.'

Chapter 47

News travelled fast.

The pilot radioed ahead to tell air-traffic control what had happened. The traffic controllers rang their wives and husbands. People ran out of their houses and told their neighbours.

All across Stanislavia, phones rang and emails arrived, delivering the good news.

Within minutes, half the people in the country had been told that Colonel Zinfandel was dead. But none of them knew whether to believe the news. Was it true? Or was it just a cruel rumour?

Thousands of people flocked to the airport, driving cars and bicycles, desperate to discover the truth. All of them wanted to ask the same questions. What had happened? Was Colonel Zinfandel dead? Was their country free of him?

People stood on the runway and stared at the sky, searching for the first sign of the president's plane.

'There!' shouted someone.

'Yes! There! Look!'

Shouts went up around the crowd. People pointed at the sky. A small dot was getting larger. The plane was coming closer.

The presidential plane landed on the runway and taxied towards the main building.

The plane stopped. A gangway came down to the ground. A door opened. A boy stepped out and stared at the huge crowd that had gathered.

Another boy emerged from the plane and stood beside him. Then a girl. And a small dog.

They blinked at the intense sunlight.

People stared back at them. No one knew what to do. They didn't recognise the boys, the girl or the dog. Who were they? Why had they emerged from the president's plane? And what had happened to him?

Max Raffifi was the first to speak. He opened his mouth and shouted at the top of his voice: 'Colonel Zinfandel is dead! Long live Stanislavia!'

For a moment, no one reacted. And then the crowd erupted in cheers and applause. Their country had suffered enough under the brutal dictatorship of Colonel Zinfandel. Now, at last, they were free.

Chapter 48

At four o'clock that afternoon, the Stanislavian State Television Service broadcast a special programme.

The whole country watched.

In bars and cafés, homes and offices, people stopped whatever they were doing and turned on the television. Everyone wanted to see the interview with the boy who had liberated their country.

The screen showed the most famous reporter in Stanislavia. She was a blonde women with fierce blue eyes and a strong chin. She looked directly into the camera and spoke in a serious tone, explaining that she was conducting the first interview with the three people who were responsible for the death of Colonel Zinfandel.

The camera showed Tim, Max and Natascha sitting together on a red sofa. They all looked nervous.

Grk was lying on the carpet at their feet. He wasn't nervous. He didn't care about the cameras, the journalists, the bright lights or the millions of people who would be watching the interview. He just closed his eyes, stretched out his legs and went to sleep.

The interviewer quizzed Max first. She asked a few questions about himself, his parents and his life. Then she invited him to describe what had happened earlier that day on the presidential plane.

Max spoke slowly, picking his words with care. He described how he and Natascha had been driven out of Paris and taken aboard the plane. He explained how Tim and Grk had followed them in a taxi, smuggled themselves aboard the plane and hidden in a cupboard for most of the flight. Then he described how Colonel Zinfandel had died.

The interviewer thanked Max for talking to her and turned to Natascha. 'You were born in Stanislavia,' she said. 'You couldn't come back here while Colonel Zinfandel was president. What are you going to do now? Are you going to stay here in Stanislavia? Or are you going to go back to London?'

'London is our home now,' said Natascha. 'We're going to go back there and finish school. And then, maybe, we'll come back to Stanislavia.'

The interviewer smiled and said, 'I hope you will.'

Finally the interviewer turned her attention to Tim. Speaking in English, she said, 'How about you, Tim? Are you planning to stay in Stanislavia?'

'No, thanks,' said Tim. 'I want to go home.'

'I'm sure you'll get exactly what you want,' said the interviewer.

And he did.

A few hours later, another plane touched down in Stanislavia, bringing Mr and Mrs Malt from London. They collected Tim, Max, Natascha and Grk, put them on the plane and took them home again.

The following morning, Tim woke up in his own bed.

He was planning to spend the whole morning there. And no one was going to stop him.

With a big smile on his face, Tim turned over, snuggled deeper into his duvet and went back to sleep.